FAST TRACK

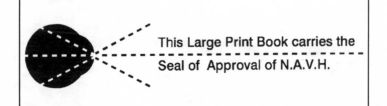

This Large Print Book carries the
Seal of Approval of N.A.V.H.

FAST TRACK

ED GORMAN

THORNDIKE PRESS

An imprint of Thomson Gale, a part of The Thomson Corporation

Detroit • New York • San Francisco • New Haven, Conn. • Waterville, Maine • London

LIBRARY OF CONGRESS CATALOGING-IN-PUBLICATION DATA

Gorman, Edward.
    Fast track / by Ed Gorman.
      p. cm. — (Thorndike Press large print western.)
    "A Dev Mallory adventure series" — T.p. verso.
    ISBN-13: 978-0-7862-9341-4 (alk. paper)
    ISBN-10: 0-7862-9341-1 (alk. paper)
    1. Horse racing — Fiction. 2. Thoroughbred horse — Fiction. 3. California
— Fiction. 4. Secret service — Fiction. 5. Large type books. I. Title.
PS3557.O759F37 2007
813'.54—dc22   2006038719

Published in 2007 by arrangement with The Berkley Publishing Group, a member of Penguin Group (USA) Inc.

Printed in the United States of America on permanent paper
10 9 8 7 6 5 4 3 2 1

This book and many others are
dedicated to Linda Siebels,
whose help is invaluable.

ONE

I don't wake up easy. I wake up, most of the time anyway, violent. I have a lot of nightmares from my somewhat bloody past, so if you have the misfortune of trying to rouse me, I just might start swinging on you even before I get my eyes open.

Which happened when the conductor started shaking me that late June afternoon in my train seat.

Fortunately, he was used to waking up drunks, so he knew how to handle people like me. He'd give me a little poke and then lean back while I tried to land a right hook on him.

"Weren't you supposed to get off in Corvair?" he asked.

I got myself sitting up, embarrassed a little about trying to punch him, dug in my short pocket for my Bull Durham and papers, and said, "Huh?"

"Your ticket. You were supposed to get off

in Corvair."

My hand was shaking for some reason, and I didn't think I'd be able to roll a smoke. I put the makings back in my pocket and said, "Yeah. I'm getting off at Corvair. Are we there now?"

"There? We're about forty miles past it."

"Why the hell didn't you wake me up?"

This was a respectable car, apparently. The people around me started hissing about my bad language. At the last transfer, I'd done my best to find an unrespectable car full of bad women and evil poker players, but I hadn't had any luck.

"Well, I saw you sleeping with that ticket to Rock Creek stuffed into your hand and —"

"Rock Creek? My ticket was for Corvair."

He nodded. "That's what I thought, too. I thought for sure your ticket said Corvair. But then I saw this" — he flashed the red ticket to Rock Creek — "and I just figured I'd made a mistake. Only reason I woke you up is because we're coming into Rock Creek in about ten minutes."

I had a taste in my mouth that had been there a few times before, as if a buzzard had nested in there. I thought I knew now what had happened.

At the last stop, I'd left my flask in my

8

bag on my seat while I got out and walked around the platform. I like fresh air and hate cramped muscles.

While I was gone, and the whole excursion was maybe ten minutes, somebody had dropped something in my flask. Probably a "shanghai," which is what they call the pill they drop into drinks in the saloons of seamen on shore leave in San Francisco. You pass out, they drag you in a back room, and you wake up at sea, a prisoner on a frigate bound for hell, if not somewhere worse. You're eventually set free after they've worked you to blood and bone. Gratis, of course.

"Well," I said, starting to feel the familiar headache and nausea that usually accompany this kind of doping, "you did what you could."

"You don't look so good," he said, and no doubt that was an understatement. "You be all right?"

"Thanks," I said. I would have nodded, but if I'd done that, my head might have rolled off my shoulder and into the aisle, and I figured I'd already shocked the respectable passengers enough for one day.

I carried a leather bag, a .44 holstered to my waist, and a stomach that threatened to escape up my windpipe at the nearest opportunity.

I realized then that my hangover from the shanghai had poked some serious holes in my memory.

I'd been traveling with a very pretty young woman who worked for the Secret Service, the Boss's previous employer before he formed, at the request of the President, the agency I work for, the agency so secret that it doesn't even have a name. Not a real one, anyway.

I walked to the farthest end of the car where the conductor was taking tickets from newly boarding passengers.

I said, "There was a woman with me."

"Yes, sir. That there was, and a fine-looking one, too, if you don't mind my saying so."

"I don't mind. Where did she go?"

He was surprised. "Why, she got off at Corvair."

"Without me?"

He gave me a look that indicated he thought I was either crazy or still drunk. I was so addled that it took me a second to figure it out. I was there, she was gone, so of course she'd gotten off without me. I felt like an idiot, so I said, "I mean, did she get off alone?"

"No, sir. She was with those two gen-

10

tlemen."

"What two gentlemen?"

He gave me another look. "The ones who took her off the train. She was awfully sick — the way you were when you woke up. They said they were taking care of her since we couldn't seem to wake you up. Said they were good friends of yours."

"Damn," I said.

"Is something wrong, sir?"

"I've been shanghaied and now she has been, too."

"I'm not sure what that means, sir. 'Shanghaied,' you say?"

"Never mind. Thank you."

That would teach her to sneak drinks from my flask.

If they didn't kill her before I was able to find her, I'd have to warn Tess O'Neill of the Secret Service about the perils of drinking.

Rock Creek turned out to be an old mining town that had somehow survived the gold running out. It was near the ocean, so it had made itself over into a tourist town where people with money could spend the summer or winter, depending on their climate preferences.

Night had turned the water inky and the

11

half-moon brilliant. The waves came in with soothing beauty, the moonshine on their surface lighting a gold pathway to the beach.

The three hotels were on the north end of the four-block business district. The main street was busy with buggies. There was a line in front of the theater advertising *Musicale Troop San Fran.* I was pretty sure they meant *Troupe,* but it would have been rude to point that out.

I found a café, drank three cups of coffee, and then went to look up Western Union. They were just closing, and the man with the fancy red mustaches didn't look happy about waiting for me to conduct my business.

I sent the Boss a wire indicating that I was missing a partner but was heading to Corvair, anyway. I made the message as cryptic as I could. You want to advertise anything, just put it down on Western Union yellow and the telegrapher will blab it all over.

Horseback would be the only way I'd be getting to Corvair. After I'd sent the telegram, I found the livery.

A crabby woman in a flannel shirt and with a pair of store-bought teeth that clicked when she spoke stood in the open barn door, hands on hips and ragging on an old man who was begging her to help him up.

12

He lay in a pile of rumpled old clothes and extended a shaky, skeletonlike hand to her.

"Shut up, Merle," she said. "We got a customer."

"I shouldn't ought to drink," the old man said mournfully. "And if you'll jes' help me up, I promise I won't do it no more."

"You're some damned husband, Merle. How many thousand times I hear you promise that in the last forty-six years, huh?"

"This time I mean it, honey pie, I truly do."

She looked up at me and snorted. " 'Honey pie.' You men think you serve up a dish of the sweets and us gals'll do anything you want." She glared down at him. "So drunk he comes here and falls on his back. And today is my birthday." She took her first good look at me. "You stayin' at one of the hotels?"

"Nope. Just want to buy a horse."

"*Buy* a horse? Where do you think you are, mister? This here's a livery. We can put animals up, even let you have one for a couple days, but I sure don't have much to sell."

"You have to have something, don't you? I need to get to Corvair."

Because the only light was a lantern hanging on the door frame behind her, I couldn't tell if I was imagining the way her expression changed suddenly or not. But it seemed to, some kind of recognition.

"You sound like you need to get there in a hurry. The race, huh?"

"Yeah. The race."

"I don't like it when them prince fellas show up American horses. He's won how many of them races now?"

"Seven. And this is the biggest one. Supposedly the best Thoroughbreds from all over America running against his Thoroughbred. Race is just five days from now."

"Well, you can make the ride there by morning on a good horse."

"That's what I figured. And that's where you come in. A good horse."

She tightened up some. Seemed nervous.

"I got to run a quick errand," she said. "I got a rope corral down by the creek. You can look over the stock down there. See somethin' you like and you're willin' to pay what I ask, the horse's all yours."

"Fine."

Then she did something that reminded me of a minstrel-show stunt, where the sober one has to deal with the drunk one. On stage, this would involve all kinds of

14

funny business. But here she just wanted to be efficient and get the old man the hell off the dirt street in front of their place of business.

She picked him up and slung him over her shoulder with easy skill. She wasn't even breathing hard as she walked back into the darkness of the livery.

I followed her inside. It wasn't a clean place — even for somebody who's been around horses his whole life like me, the acid stench of horseshit was overpowering — but at least it was orderly. I didn't stumble over any shovels or rakes, anyway.

All the stalls but one were full with horses of different breeds. One at the end was empty, and it was into this one that she threw her husband without any particular care about where he would land. I heard his groan when he hit the ground.

His wife ignored the sound. She turned to me as if nothing had happened and said, "You go down toward the creek now and look at them horses in the corral. I'll be back in five, ten minutes."

Her voice was tight, and she scratched nervously on her right jaw. I kept wondering about that expression I thought I'd seen. I sensed that something was wrong here. Maybe it was as simple as her being embarrassed and upset by her husband's being drunk. Maybe it was something a lot more important.

There were six horses in the corral. It wasn't hard to make a decision. The cayuse was the one I wanted. Those Indian ponies had an easy seat and plenty of endurance. I led her out of the corral. The cool breeze off the wide creek just below us had started to revive me. I looked up at the stars on this fine gentle night and felt a good kind of loneliness, satisfied for the moment to be alive and a tiny part of the vast darkness.

But the longer I stood there, my right hand resting on the neck of the cayuse, the more I realized that something was wrong in this situation. The old woman had recognized me somehow, or she'd heard about me. That's the expression I'd seen in her face. And the errand she'd run was to tell somebody I was in town — somebody who'd played some part in shanghaiing my flask.

I took the cayuse up to the livery barn and looked around for a saddle. I was partial to the Cheyenne style because that was the type I'd used when I'd worked on the ranch after the war. Tonight I had to settle for one that looked as if it might have been ordered out of a Sears catalog.

I was still looking for a saddle when I felt something jab the middle of my back.

"You don't go stealin' from us, bub."

The old man sounded pretty damned sober now. Some drunks can recover pretty fast to a point of semi-sobriety when something important happens. He thought I was stealing from him.

"I was going to leave you money."

"Sure you were. You looked like a slicker the minute I laid eyes on you. Now you turn around here and face me."

I did what he asked, but I did it a lot faster than he'd expected. Before he was able to get a shot off, I hunched down and threw myself at his waist, staggering him back a good five feet. The repeater flew from his hands and hit the sandy soil without firing.

He was wobbling, about to go over backward. I grabbed him by the front of his shirt and threw him against the wall of the livery with a heavy thump. I grabbed his shirt again and hauled him outside into the fresh air away from the barn.

"Where'd your wife go, old man?"

"How the hell would I know?"

The way he smelled, I might as well have been holding an outhouse. He was bonier than I thought. His eyes gleamed with panic and rummy confusion.

17

Then I had my knife out. I put the tip of the blade right against his right eyelid, which closed automatically when the blade got within a few inches of the eyeball itself.

"You know how fast I could kill you, old man?"

He started whimpering. All his whiskey resolve was gone. Now he wasn't worried about his money. He was worried about his miserable life. Not to mention his eyeball.

I could hear him pissing his pants, the sound sickening in the silence.

Now he was crying. "It wasn't me. It was Ida. She made the deal with the man."

"What man?"

"He told her he was federal."

"Bullshit."

I eased the point of the blade a little harder against his eyelid.

"It's true! It's true! Jesus! He told her what you'd look like and that you'd be needin' a horse. And that she was s'posed to run and tell him when you got here."

Then I heard her. She had an unmistakable voice.

She was walking into the livery.

"He must still be down to the corral, looking them horses over."

"I'll handle it from here, Ida. You just stay up here till it's all over."

She must have looked in the stall where she'd thrown her husband. "I wonder where old Merle went."

I was at most twenty feet from the back of the livery. I had just enough time to get the cayuse and get out of here, but I knew I wasn't going anywhere, not until I found out what was going on.

I let go of the old man, and he dragged himself back to the livery, where he disappeared into the deeper shadows of the interior.

The man with Ida came out of the livery. He was a dapper little bastard in a dark suit, with a celluloid collar, a wide dark cravat, and something I doubted you saw much in this area: spats.

He flipped a gold coin off his thumb as he approached me. He did this without ever looking at the coin or his hand. It would land on his palm and he'd flip it right back up again. It flashed in the moonlight as it tumbled through the air.

Ida was right behind him. She said, "You scared the hell out of my husband, mister." Glaring at me.

"Get out of here," the little man told her.

"He didn't have no call to do it," she snapped.

The man looked at her, and she went back

to the barn.

"They'll be waiting for you in Corvair," Spats said. "The Hotel Royale. The name you want is Franklin Givens. Room 202."

"He has the girl?"

"He knows where the girl is. You'll get her back after you talk to him."

"She's federal, you know. You boys didn't think this through."

"Oh, we thought it through, all right. And that's why we did it. We're going to make a whole lot of money on that race, and you're going to help us."

"Yeah? And how would that be?"

"We'll go to a saloon and talk about that."

"Go ahead and give me an idea."

"The horse Starcrossed, the one everybody says is going to win?" Another smile for me. "You're going to poison him for us."

TWO

Right here I should tell you about the Boss. The blue glass eye in the right socket? Happened on a steamboat when a Confederate saw the Boss breaking into a passenger room. It's one of those manly stories that I'd doubt coming from anyone else of the male persuasion. The way the Boss tells it, he was so angry about his eye being ripped out with a knife that he tore the other man's eyes out with his own fingers, smashed the man's head against a pillar until the man was dead, and then threw him overboard. The Boss opted for a glass eye instead of an eyepatch.

The Boss held many jobs in our government over the years.

During the war he worked for the Secret Service. Few people seem to know, or care, that the Secret Service is in charge of investigating counterfeit money operations. During the war, on both sides, maybe as

21

much as fifty percent of all paper currency was queer. This could have proved fatal to either side.

I spent most of the war setting up counterfeit schemes for a friend of mine named Phil Darcy, who was a subcabinet officer in the Lincoln Administration. We'd been roommates at Dartmouth. We'd also spent seven months together on three different cattle drives, dropping out of college for a year so we could learn to be cowboys. We wanted to prove — mostly to ourselves — what manly young men we were. At the start, we gave the cowboys some pretty good laughs, I'm sure. But after a couple of months, we started catching on. We "rode drag," as they call it, and doubled our weight in dust alone. Try riding behind a couple hundred head of cattle sometime and you'll see what I mean. The dust gets so heavy you have to wear a bandanna the same way you have to in a sandstorm. I broke an arm getting thrown off a horse, two fingers when I got them caught in a rope, and I still have a knot just above my ear from one of the many fistfights I'd gotten into. Cowboys seem to think that beating the shit out of each other is a good way to pass the time.

Phil's father was a good friend of several important men and got us our jobs with the

Secret Service. This was after the war, following a time when I did a little counterfeiting on my own. Then I managed to survive a marriage to a woman who murdered her adulterous lover and somehow convinced me I should help her be found innocent. I never said I was smart. After the lady, surviving a war sounded easy. Another friend of mine from the war introduced me to the Boss and I was hired for my present job.

By then the Boss was working for another agency, the one that didn't have a name, the one that the Congressmen appropriated money for, but didn't even know existed. A job with the Boss promised to provide interesting work, and it surely did.

Nearly fifteen years of assignments led up to the present one, which the Boss had explained to me this way: "There's this small country called Worthingham. It's an island near Scotland. The State Department wants to stay on its good side because Scotland seems to fight us a lot about policy matters. If you know anything about Thoroughbred racing, you know that Starcrossed is supposedly the fastest horse in the world. Prince John Brean owns the horse, and he's running it in two weeks in a race in Corvair, California. For the biggest purse in history.

"The racing facilities there are bigger than anything on the East Coast. But I don't have to tell a cynical bastard like you about horse racing, do I? It's the most corrupt sport in the world. And especially in this country. Hell, it's gotten so bad that Congress is thinking of banning it altogether."

We both had to smile a little at the idea of Congress calling something else corrupt. But whores love to put on the airs of innocence.

But the Boss never smiled for long, which was just as well. He didn't have the face for it. On him a smile was downright scary. He said, "The State Department has convinced the President that it's in the national interest to see that nothing happens to Starcrossed or the prince. We put a trainer we selected in there — a man named Jake Duncan — and we're working closely with the leading stockholder in the track, a man named Carter Steffens. Got that?"

I'd worked with Jake before, but I didn't see any need to slow the Boss down by answering. So I just nodded, and he went right on talking.

"To give you some hint of what you're walking into, seven men have been killed in gunfights involving bets since the track opened in 1880. And it's estimated that one fourth to one third of the races have been fixed in one way or another. Steffens is clean, as far as we know. Besides being the chief stockholder, he's the general manager of the track; he's run for governor three times and lost, but that hasn't humbled him. When he was young, he played football and did some boxing. He was pretty good at both, and there are plenty of stories about his ability to crack heads in barroom brawls. Rough-and-tumble. Not what you might expect from a fifty-five-year-old from wine country, but we're talking about California. The only rules out there are that there aren't any rules. Got that?"

I nodded again.

"Good. But tough as he is, and as smart as he is, Steffens can't stop all kinds of thugs and crooked trainers and crooked jockeys and crooked horse doctors from fixing the races. That's just the way of things. And that's where you come in."

"I'm going to stop someone from fixing the race?"

He looked at me for a minute to see if I was sassing him. He must have decided I wasn't, or else he didn't think it was worth commenting on. This time.

"You're there just to worry about Starcrossed," he said. "He's the big draw. We've convinced both the prince and Steffens that with the agents we've assigned there to guard the horse, he'll be completely safe. While the men are guarding the animal, we want you to mix in with the crowd and see if you spot any familiar faces. We've got a whole book of information on the men who work on fixing races. I want you to spend a day with the book and then head out to Corvair.

"Oh, and one more thing. The President thinks you and that Tess O'Neill have done some good work together. So she'll be traveling along with you. You understand all this, Dev? If anything happens to the prince or that horse — don't even bother coming back here to Washington. Because your career will be over. Got that?"

In case you hadn't noticed, the Boss likes the phrase "Got that?" And when he uses it, he doesn't really expect an answer. If you're not the type who gets it the first time, you wouldn't be working for him. So I just nodded again and took the book he handed me.

So now here I sat in a saloon across from a man who was one of Tess O'Neill's kidnappers, and he was telling me how I was going to poison the most famous racehorse on the

26

planet. If, that is, I had any interest in getting Tess O'Neill back alive.

"You'll be given something they had some scientist work up back East," the little man in the fancy duds said. He hadn't offered a name. Why bother? It would be made up, anyway. "He says that nobody will ever be able to trace it."

"Who says?"

"The man you're going to meet at the Hotel Royale." He paused as if trying to remember the name, which of course was a false one. "Franklin Givens."

"And if I take this 'something' the scientist worked up for you, what will I be doing with it?" I asked.

"A simple little job. You'll be able to get close to the horse. Everybody will trust you. Just mix the stuff in with the feed, and that'll be the end of Starcrossed."

"There'll be an investigation."

"Sure there will." He laughed. "You don't think we're dumb, do you? The head of the investigating board is on our payroll. Besides, who's going to suspect that a government agent, the very man who's protecting the horse, would poison it?"

"And people say horse racing is crooked. I can't understand why."

He smirked. "Come on now, you're a

smart man. Everything's crooked, when you look at it close enough. Hell, churches are crooked. When I was growin' up, we had this pastor who'd pocket a good share of the Sunday tithing. You know what he was doing with it? He had two different gals he kept in Kansas City. He'd go in there a couple times a week. Fella must've been sixty. He must've had a machine in his pants, keepin' two young women like that satisfied."

"Maybe he didn't keep them satisfied, you ever think of that?"

He waved me off "Nah, at the trial they both gave him a lot of compliments. One of 'em even told a reporter that our rev was hung like a horse. She put it nicer than that, but you see what I'm getting at."

"There's a lot of things that could go wrong with your plan."

"Well, if anything does go wrong, that pretty partner of yours will be deader than Starcrossed is supposed to be." He lifted his beer mug in salute. "To our mutual success — we get the money, you get the girl."

Ten minutes later, we left the saloon and started walking back down toward the livery. This time, with him along, I expected no trouble from the owners, and there was none.

I had a small surprise for my new friend, though. He watched me get my horse; he watched me saddle her; and then he watched me walk over to where he stood slightly upslope from where I'd gotten the cayuse all set up.

For a grifter, he was pretty damned trusting. He let me get so close that when I hit him in the stomach I broke at least one of his ribs. Then he had no choice but to let me break his nose.

I didn't feel as satisfied as I'd hoped to.

And it turned out I shouldn't have. The hotel where he told me I'd find Franklin Givens? He wasn't there, nor was anybody who could tell me a damn thing about him or Tess.

THREE

If there were such a thing as reincarnation, I'd have to give serious consideration to coming back as a famous racehorse. A staff of sixteen worked on Starcrossed every day. He was fed, groomed, walked, examined, rested, photographed, applauded, and had his sperm bragged on the same way you hear saloon lover-boys brag on their prowess with women. Not a bad job when you think about it. Especially when you start thinking about the stud services that come along with retirement.

And on top of that, you got to bedazzle folks. Not many of us get to bedazzle folks even once in our lives, but Starcrossed did it often. And then he got to bask in people's adulation. I wondered what that would be like, but I had a feeling I wasn't ever going to find out.

Early every morning, just like this morning, a groom would meet up with Starcrossed on the track and the bedazzlement would begin. The adulation was there, too, but there wasn't as much of it as there would be after a big race, not when you were the winner.

Having never been much for gambling, I had no idea of how much time, patience, and money were expended on racing Thoroughbreds like Starcrossed. I had even less sense of their grace, beauty, power, and speed.

I did know, because the prince had told me, that all Thoroughbreds were descended from three horses that were called the *foundation sires,* and that Starcrossed's ancestry could be traced back to one of them known as the Byerly Turk, a horse that had been brought to England from Hungary around two hundred years ago. Beyond that, all I knew, really, was that they had pretty good lives.

"How come you're all dressed like cowboys?" an Eastern reporter asked. He was dressed like what he was, a city boy, but he didn't look out of place. There were all kinds at the track.

"That's because we *are* cowboys," Jake Duncan said, winking at me. Jake was the trainer the Boss had planted at the racetrack in Corvair. I'd met most of the other trainers and all the principals. I'd been here a full day now.

And of course I'd known Jake before. He was a damned good trainer, and I'd sometimes wondered how he ever got hooked up with the Boss, though I'd never asked. He'd come to this country from Scotland when his wife died, and somehow he'd found his way into the Boss's employ. He was a racetrack genius who preferred animals to people, which suited the Boss just fine. He was one of those jaunty men who knew as much about horse medicine as most vets and who loved horses with a passion that was occasionally embarrassing.

"But horse people back East don't dress like cowboys," the reporter persisted. He'd arrived about the time I had yesterday with his fancy naïve questions and we were already sick of him.

"Well, maybe they should start," Jake said. "Maybe their horses would run better if they dressed right."

That was Jake. He enjoyed playing the role of the tough, impatient horse trainer. And he could afford to.

The reporter frowned and walked away.

And it was just then that one of Jake's men brought Starcrossed on to the track.

This was the animal that belonged to the

man the State Department wanted to keep happy.

Jake's job was to prepare the animal to race for the biggest purse in history just four days from now, June 11, 1884.

As I watched Jake this beautiful morning, so soon after dawn that you could see your breath and enjoy air that smelled of snow-capped mountains and pine forests, I didn't know that he would be murdered that night. Had I known I would have hustled him the hell out of there.

At the moment, he was just a tough little man in his late forties who rarely dressed in anything except a denim shirt and jeans, and who had an almost supernatural knowledge of his animals.

Jake's rider that morning, a groom named Gilpin, led Starcrossed past the early morning crowd. There was a buzz of voices, and I could almost feel the anticipation in the air.

Starcrossed had a big, wide chest and skinny legs. He looked around as if he knew he owned the place. His morning exercise would consist of his being galloped around the track and then walked by a groom while he cooled down.

"I'm sure going to miss him when this is over," a female voice said

Amanda, Jake's daughter, slipped in next to me at the fence where we stood watching Starcrossed. Amanda was barely twenty. No matter how many fancy ladies came to the race — and there would be many and they would be fancy indeed — I doubted that any of them would look any better than Amanda.

Her mother had died when she was five, so Jake had raised her. He'd brought her over from Scotland with him fifteen years ago. She didn't have his accent, but she certainly had his horse sense and his almost religious devotion to horses.

And she wasn't just tagging along to see the race. She'd been with Jake ever since he was assigned to Starcrossed, working as a groom. She'd worked with Jake most of her life, in fact, and knew almost as much about training horses as he did.

Despite her pretty little face, she was very much like her father. Tough as hell when she needed to be. She was already a good trainer; someday she'd be a great one like her old man. The one difference was that the denim shirt and jeans she wore were filled out much more attractively than Jake's.

"We talking about the horse or the prince?" I said.

Jake chuckled, knowing what I was talking about. Hard to say which of her crushes was more serious, the one she had on Starcrossed or the one she had on Prince John Brean.

"They're both real sensitive and kind of high-strung," Jake said. "Royalty's like that."

Amanda was about to give him an argument about his comments when another voice said, "Hi, Amanda."

Prince John had a cousin. His name was Richard Caldwell, and he was the third point of the triangle — Amanda loved John, and Richard loved Amanda, but Amanda didn't love Richard. All this had been set in motion before I got here — a perfect stage meller-drama. Except these were real people with real feelings.

Richard was overweight with sandy hair already thinning on top. He wasn't quite twenty. His eyes were always watery, and he tugged at his lower lip so often you wanted to slap his hand away. He wore a light-blue Western shirt that didn't hang right on his fleshy torso and a pair of baggy dungarees that fit him worse than the shirt did.

He was one of those kids who reminded me of the irritating chubby little puppy who follows you all day long and you can't get rid of. And when you do kick out gently and tell him to go find his rightful owner, you feel guilty about it.

"Hi, Dev," he said.

"Morning, Richard."

"Hi, Jake."

But Jake was looking over Richard's shoulder.

Walking toward us now, dressed like landed gentry in a tight hunting jacket and tight trousers tucked into riding boots, came Donald Sterling, who was Starcrossed's official trainer. He was some kind of vague English royalty, an earl or one of those. He'd been with the prince and Starcrossed since the birth of the Thoroughbred. But when John saw how much better his horse responded to Jake than to Sterling, he'd eased Sterling aside.

Jake and Sterling pretended to be civil. But the tension between them was such that even when you were twenty feet away you could feel it.

"I don't suppose you'd like a little piece of advice, would you, old boy?" Sterling said to Jake.

Jake grinned. "No, 'old boy,' I don't suppose I would."

Amanda glanced at her father. She looked apprehensive, too. It probably would have been better for these two middle-aged men

36

to just throw a few punches at each other and get it over with. This ruse of getting along was one hell of a slow way to die.

Sterling looked at the only one of us he considered a peer.

"Richard, if you would be so kind, would you tell Jake here that he shouldn't have cut back on how much salt is put in Starcrossed's water? He needs it for digestion."

Jake said: "Richard, if you would be so kind, would you tell His Royal Highness here that right now we have a bigger problem with his dehydration than we do his digestion?"

This carping would have gone on for some time, but something happened that made their mutual dislike for each other irrelevant.

Starcrossed was spooked. He was bucking wildly up and down, his front hooves coming dangerously close to striking the rail. He could easily be doing serious, even permanent, damage to himself. Gilpin had lost all control.

Jake took off running faster than you would think a man his age could manage.

He burst on to the track, running headlong toward his horse. Amanda followed, hurrying to keep up with him.

The press would be telling tales of this

moment for decades to come, and the men who witnessed it would be telling it just as long, one saloon at a time. The day the most celebrated horse of his time went loco on everybody. But which ending would make a better story? The horse finally regains its senses and is taken harmlessly off the track? Or the horse savages itself and maybe the rider in the process and can never race again?

Jake was fearless.

Starcrossed continued bucking, pausing only to turn himself to a slightly different angle. This gave everybody the false hope that he had settled down. But then he went right back to bucking, forcing Gilpin to go through all his tricks to restrain a wild horse. None of which happened to work at the moment. After a second or two more, he gave up. It was all he could do to hang on.

Jake waited until his horse had all four hooves on the track and was ready to turn to a different angle — and then he moved. He grabbed the reins to steady Starcrossed as much as he could, and then shouted something I couldn't hear from that distance.

Whatever he'd shouted caused Gilpin to pitch himself off Starcrossed. He hit on his feet, almost fell, then took off at a staggering run to get away from the horse.

In the few seconds before the horse started bucking again, Jake pulled himself up into the saddle and then threw his arms around the animal's neck.

He started talking to the horse at the precise moment Starcrossed set himself to start bucking again. It was almost as if Jake was whispering in his ear.

And Starcrossed was listening. There was a furtive, halfhearted buck, one that looked almost comical, as if it were a show-horse trick that had failed, followed by a shuddering step to the side, and then the animal stood quietly, breathing a little heavily, maybe, but otherwise looking as if nothing had happened.

But something had happened, all right. Jake had saved Starcrossed from hurting himself, maybe even destroying himself, and everyone there knew it.

FOUR

The trainers work out a complete schedule for their animals, setting times when the animal needs to trot or gallop or jog. Twice a day they check the horse for injuries, infection, any kind of illness. They even know, the good ones anyway, when the horse needs to relax, when he's sluggish or skittish because of fatigue or the pressure everybody around him is putting on him.

The great trainers, like Jake, pretty much run the show. They know which jockeys to hire, and they know which people they want as staff when they're in their home stable. Some trainers go so far as to make up a short list of people who are to be allowed around the animal. Sometimes this list even excludes the owner or members of his family the trainer thinks irritate or unnerve the horse.

Until the Boss ordered me here, I'd thought of horses as being good for riding and not much else, but I'd learned a lot in a hurry. And I already knew a lot about horses. I'd had horses I'd felt close to, and horses that put me into a funk when they had to be put down. And I'd had horses I dreamed of sending off a cliff.

All this meant that I had a pretty good idea of what everybody around Starcrossed must have been feeling. The world's most celebrated racehorse doesn't usually behave so oddly. It was probably just some kind of fluke, or so they thought. I wasn't so sure about that, myself. But whatever had happened, it had to have left everybody scared.

Over the next ten minutes, Jake took his animal back to the nearby stables, and Prince John Brean himself appeared in the company of the track general manager, Carter Steffens, the man who owned eighty percent of the track and never let you forget it. The Boss hadn't warned me that although we were "working closely with him," he was a thoroughgoing sonofabitch.

The gossip had already started. Jockeys and their mounts had already started their daily workouts while owners and other trainers speculated on what had just happened with Starcrossed.

Donald Sterling said: "I tried to tell Jake that he shouldn't have changed the salt content."

It was hard for me to imagine that was the trouble here, and only Richard gave Sterling the satisfaction of an answer. "You really think that was the reason Starcrossed acted that way?"

Amanda put a hand on the boy's shoulder. "Oh, Richard. Sterling's just mad because he isn't the trainer now. Salt didn't have anything to do with this."

"Then why'd he say it?"

"Because he'll do anything to make my dad look bad." She stared right at Sterling. "Right, Sterling?"

Sterling returned the tart remark. "The queen will never accept you. She has her heart set on John marrying Liz."

And with that he left.

Liz was Elizabeth Hawes. She was the English beauty traveling with her mother independent of John's group. But she'd made it clear, especially to Amanda, that she considered Amanda nothing more than an infatuation on John's part.

One more cast member in this meller-drama.

I wasn't entirely sure how the prince felt about all this. That he hadn't fallen in love with the red-haired Amanda was testimony to how many women were constantly hovering around him, wanting for royal favors.

"There's the bitch now," Amanda said, under her breath so that only I heard her.

And when I glanced to my right, smiling at Amanda's use of the language, I saw Liz and her mother sitting in a box in one of the best seats in the entire grandstand.

Liz, an ash-blonde of cold beauty, glared at Amanda and then turned her attention back to the woman who had bestowed that beauty on her. Mrs. Davinia Hawes, who was at this moment fanning herself with a racing circular. Her husband, Liz's father, had died several years earlier and had left her and her daughter with an immense fortune that they were enjoying by traveling wherever Prince John might be going.

The two women, twins but for weight and a few wrinkles, took that moment to will us out of existence. We could have set ourselves on fire and they wouldn't have looked.

There are men you really want to dislike. Feel even that you *should* dislike for the sake of the world being a right and just place.

Prince John Brean was one of those young blond men who actually looked pretty natural with a dumb crown on his head. He could have stood in for a book cover where the Knights of the Round Table were posing in chain mail with broadswords. The only thing that redeemed his wealth, his royalty, his looks, and his intelligence was the fact that he took care to pretend that he was unaware of all the gifts he'd accrued purely by cosmic chance. He was a hell of a lot more cordial and more patient than most young men in his position would be. I was just uncomfortable with the whole notion of the Divine Right of Kings, a so-called right that was nothing more than chance as far as I was concerned — just the right sperm traveling up the right tube in the right woman.

The word from Jake was that John, as the prince liked to be called, had turned into a pretty fair ranch hand since he'd come to America. He'd read a good number of dime novels in his native land and decided that he'd give up the life of a spoiled pretty boy, at least for a short time, and become a true Westerner. He'd come over five months early so he could learn about the Western way of life.

And he hadn't just played at being a ranch hand. He'd learned the real business. He'd put in time baling hay, riding fence, scrubbing down barns, and taking a turn in service at the chuck wagon on a small cattle drive, where he'd whipped up some kind of

Celtic soup that left three cowhands with the kind of diarrhea that makes death seem like a pleasant alternative. He'd learned how to use a gun without injuring himself or anybody else; how to ford a river with horse in tow; and how to tell the difference between a playful bear and a mean-ass one. The story was that he'd initially chosen the wrong bear to pard up with and damned near got his throat ripped out for the mistake.

He was, at twenty-two, in the parlance of commoners like myself, a decent young man. Not his fault that he'd had all those gifts lavished on him. Still, you had to blame him just a little or you wouldn't be human. Couldn't I have at least one castle?

Right now the prince and Steffens were interrogating Amanda. She looked and sounded nervous.

"I don't know, John," she said. "There wasn't any warning, was there, Dev?"

"I wasn't watching," I said. "I was talking to you."

I could see her disappointment in my words. She wanted me to back her up.

"But I'll tell you," I continued, "there couldn't have been more than a minute pass between the time he got on the track and the time he started acting up."

Steffens, in his usual horsey attire including sport coat, jodhpurs, knee-high boots, bowler, and leather gloves, scowled at me. "Don't forget, John. Mallory here isn't a horseman. He's just here to make sure Starcrossed isn't cheated in some way."

There was a lot more to it than that, of course, but the Boss hadn't seen fit to tell Steffens everything. He never told anybody everything. Not even me. Which sometimes caused complications that I thought were unnecessary.

"I think you should go see Jake," I said to the prince. "He'll have a better idea of what's going on."

"Poor Jake," John said. "He's got as much at stake here as we do." He smiled at Amanda. "He's by far the best trainer Starcrossed has ever had."

"This is all very nice," Steffens snapped. "But I want to find out what the hell happened to Starcrossed. One of the jockeys who saw it told me he looked loco."

I almost smiled at his use of "loco," which was, after all, a Western word. Coming from the mouth of a rich grandee who tried very hard to pass himself off as an Eastern grandee when he'd been born in Kansas City — it was one of the few things he'd ever done that struck me as amusing.

"That's a good idea," John said. "Let's go see Jake. Maybe he's figured it out by now."

John doffed his sweat-stained cowboy hat, Steffens just scowled, and then they were gone.

Amanda looked up at me and said, "I wish I could say the word that comes into my mind every time I'm around Steffens." She laughed. "But Dad raised me better than that."

I thought about what she'd said when she saw Liz Hawes, and smiled. Amanda asked what was so funny, but I didn't tell her.

FIVE

I did my morning check of the stables. While I wasn't directly responsible for the guards, I wanted to make sure that they were doing what they'd been hired to.

There were six guards per shift, four shifts a day. By now, they knew who I was. I'd made sure of that. I went to each entrance on the stables and checked to see that the guards were positioned to handle two entrances apiece. Anybody who wanted into the stables had to wear a small red ribbon on his shirt or blouse. He also had to have a buff-blue card with his name signed on it. Right below that name Steffens had signed his. Each visitor had to sign in and out in a long notebook that fit in the guard's back pocket.

Everybody was still thinking about Starcrossed's odd behavior. Those who wanted the horse to win the purse were worried. Those who wanted the horse to lose were hopeful this was a sign of sure weakness.

Steffens came over to me while I was winding up my check. For once, he didn't bring a sneer. He brought a brow-knitted worried look.

"That episode we saw earlier wasn't good."

"If you mean Starcrossed, no, I don't suppose it was."

"The whole idea is that he's superior to all the other horses. That way, if he's defeated, it'll seem almost like a miracle."

"I suppose you're right."

"Those bastards from the papers'll be all over this. They'll start implying that he isn't the champion everybody thinks he is. But you know and I know that that's bullshit. Every horse throws a fit once in a while — just like humans do."

I was tempted to smile politely and point out that he himself threw enough tantrums for any twenty people. But being the high-minded gent I am, I said nothing.

Then our good friend Sterling was with us. One thing about even minor royalty. They are well-tutored in the art of looking superior.

"I assume you're talking about what happened to Starcrossed," he said with obvious distaste. "I warned you, Steffens, not to let

49 Middlebury Community
Public Library

the prince put Jake in charge. He's good with horses, no doubt. But Starcrossed isn't just another horse. He's the champion of the century. You'll forgive me for saying this, but a common trainer won't do. And that's what I tried to tell you."

I said: "We were just saying that all horses have times like these."

"Not champions."

"Of course champions," Steffens said. "I've been in the racing business most of my life. I've seen champions that you damned near had to push across the finish line."

Sterling shook his head condescendingly. "I should've known you two would be standing here trying to convince each other that what happened to Starcrossed this morning was just a fluke." He directed his sneer at Steffens. "You've got a lot more to lose than just money, Steffens. You've got your reputation to lose. What if it comes out that you and Mallory here — Mallory, who knows nothing about horses, even the common ones you run here, Steffens — conspired to have me removed and replaced by a man clearly my inferior? How would you like to see that in the papers? You will, too, if you see Starcrossed having any more of these so-called 'episodes.' "

And with that, having imparted his wisdom and inflicted his arrogance, he was gone.

And so, obviously shaken by Sterling's words, was Steffens.

I was headed toward the river when Jake caught up with me. The much-punched face was never really friendly unless he smiled. He had a long history of brawls, which was strange for a man who was not only a teetotaler, but who'd preach against John Barleycorn every chance he got. Amanda had explained that her father came from a long line of drinkers. He'd sworn never to take up the bottle himself. But that didn't stop him from fighting, something he seemed to enjoy. I'd seen him go after a few of the cowboys. For a man his age he was a damned hellion.

"Something's going on, Dev."

"You mean with Starcrossed?"

"Yeah."

"You think he's been doped?"

"I don't know. But that isn't all." He shook his head. "You know a man named Mitch Clarey?"

I thought it over and then said, "I've heard of him."

"Red-haired man. Kind of shifty-eyed.

Owned a string of horses out here. Good ones. He'd win a lot of races. The word was he doped a lot of the competition. But nobody could ever prove it. I was talking to one of the hot walkers and he saw this Clarey fella, and then he said he saw him last night hiding up in the grandstand with a pair of field glasses. From the angle it appeared he was looking at the stables. Like maybe he had something in mind with them. He's here today, too."

Clarey's name had been one of those in the book the Boss had given me to study. He was known to be a fixer, but he'd never been caught at it. Which meant that he was good at what he did and that when he made a mistake, he always had someone lined up to take the fall for him.

So far, he was the only person from the book who'd turned up, but I knew there were plenty of sharpers around, whether they'd been in the book or not. That was the way of it when you were working with grifters and criminals of any stripe. You could be sure that new ones would turn up all the time.

The report of Clarey's mysterious behavior made me think of Tess O'Neill. She was still missing.

"You say he's here now?" I asked Jake. "I

think I'd like to talk to him."

"He's a slicker, Dev. He's one of the biggest fixers on the West Coast but he's never spent so much as an hour in jail. And believe me, from what I've heard about him, a lot of people have tried to put him there."

"I know about that. Where'd you see him last?"

"He was over by the grandstand. Talking to his crowd. Rich people like to be seen with him. Think it looks dangerous. The young ones especially; you know, hang out with criminals because they think it makes them seem tough. He eventually nicks every one of them for a good share of money, but they're too damn stupid to see it coming." He paused. Then: "I saw you and Steffens talking to Sterling. I imagine he was telling Steffens I'm doing a bad job."

"Who the hell cares what he thinks? Steffens hates him, anyway."

"I wouldn't even be here except for the Boss. I didn't take his damn job away from him. The Boss arranged that with the prince's old man." He gave me that sharp Scots grin. "Of course, I don't really mind all that much workin' with the best Thoroughbred racer in the world."

I laughed. "Yeah, I kinda figured that wouldn't bother you a whole bunch."

"I'll tell you, Dev, what happened here this morning wasn't natural. Somebody did something. I don't know who or what but if Clarey's involved, then I'm pretty sure it involves doping. Fact is, you can almost bet on it."

I had two people I wanted to find — the mysterious Mr. Givens and the con man Clarey.

The first place I went was back to the Hotel Royale. Maybe I'd have better luck this time talking to a different desk clerk.

Today's desk clerk was a short man with his black hair parted in the middle and slicked down on both sides with some kind of grease that made it shine in the sunlight. He gave me a hard look that was supposed to let me know he was tough.

"A Mr. Givens, please."

"I don't believe we have a guest by that name," he said. He was one of those people who gulped when he lied. Gulped and looked furtive.

"The hell you say."

There must have been a threat in my tone, or maybe he saw something in my face. He took a step back, though he was already behind the counter, and said, "Yes. I do say. Sir."

He was small, and he might even have been tough. But he wasn't fast. Before he could move again, I'd gone halfway over the counter and grabbed a fistful of his shirt-front.

I slid back off the counter pulling him along so that his feet didn't touch his side of the floor. He was kicking his feet and grabbing for my wrist, but I had a tight hold and he wasn't going to escape it. I let him kick for a second or two. When I'd had enough of that, I said, "I'm going to count to ten. If you haven't told me where Givens is by then, I'm going to pull out my .44 and shoot your right ear off. Unless I miss and hit you in the eye."

He clamped his teeth together and set his mouth in a thin line, so I shook him a little before I started to count.

"One. Two. Three."

His expression didn't change. To encourage him, I drew the pistol and pointed it at his head. He took one look down the long barrel and said, "Mr. Givens isn't here. He left earlier."

I cocked the hammer.

"That's the truth! His wife wasn't feeling well, and they left. She hadn't been well since they arrived. I tried to give him the name of a good doctor, but he wouldn't listen."

He sounded truthful enough, but I wasn't sure I believed him.

"Why didn't you just tell me that in the first place?"

"Because he told me not to tell anyone he'd left."

"How much did he pay you?"

He clamped his lips together again, but I didn't really care about the amount of the bribe. I let go of his shirt and shoved him back. He didn't try anything, so I took the hammer off cock.

"What did the woman look like?"

He gave a not-bad description of Tess O'Neill.

"And you say she wasn't feeling well?"

"That's right. She seemed weak and drowsy."

The bastard who'd taken her had probably forced more drugs on her to keep her docile. Knowing Tess, they'd have had to do that. But that didn't explain why they'd left.

"What about the man?" I said.

"He was feeling just fine."

I cocked the pistol again.

"I don't mean to sass you," the clerk said, holding up his hands in front of him, as if he thought they'd stop a bullet. "I didn't get a good look at him. He kept his hat pulled down over his face, and he didn't ever look straight at me."

"You remember something, though."

"Well, I did see the back of his neck when he left. He's tall and thin. I think he had red hair."

When I finally saw the red-haired man I took to be Clarey, the fixer, he was leaving the track, just then lashing his roan into action. By the time I got to where he'd been, he was long gone.

I decided to see how the rodeo was coming along. On the morning of the race, the area inside the oval track would be used for the rodeo. Then the track would be cleaned up and made ready for the race in the afternoon.

I spent the next hour down near the river where a corral had been set up so the cowboys could walk through their various rodeo stunts. The more I was around race-track people, the more I wanted to be around the cowboys. They were, for the most part, hardworking, reasonably honest people.

Even though I'd spent time before and after the war working as a ranch hand and riding on a couple cattle drives, and even though I had the scars and broken bones to show for it, I didn't claim to be a cowpoke. But I did know the satisfaction of the open range and the beauty of sleeping under the stars — beauty, that is, when it doesn't rain, snow, or freeze your balls off. But on a nice summer night, when the mosquitoes retire early and the rattlers stay away from the campsite, there's a simple peace to be had that clears the mind and settles the soul. All the bullshit city irritations and treacheries are gone for the course of the night.

The rodeo riders had been warned about limiting the violent events. There would be no bull-riding and no bareback bronc-riding. The genteel rich folks such as Steffens had thrown in with the recent editorials in big-city newspapers that rodeos only presented the West "not as a progressive part of the United States, but an unappealing area where rowdyism and hooliganism ran rampant."

Because this was an international event, Steffens was determined to put on a small rodeo before the horse race to show the foreign visitors something "authentic" from the American West. But he wasn't going to risk anything that would offend a dowager or the big-city papers.

As Hal Macklin, the "star" of this particular rodeo, put it, "That is chickenshit on toast." But his opinion carried no weight with Steffens.

The events that *would* take place included calf-roping, steer-roping, saddle bronc-riding with "outlaw" horses excluded, team roping, plus the usual trick riding and trick roping. There would of course be clowns, who'd been hired locally, as had the extra hands for staging the rodeo.

Everybody worked through his job pretty much without any hitch. The best of the ropers, a tough-looking fleshy man named "Boots" Donovan, came over to the corral fence to stand beside me and found a place for his own elbows to rest. The nickname came from the expensive boots he wore. Ranch hands and cowboys don't make much money, but Donovan was a saver. He saved until he could get hand-tooled boots made just the way he liked them.

Donovan was one of six cowboys who earned extra pay by working nights guarding the stables. I had to admit that Steffens paid them well. He didn't want any possible harm to come to the horses.

"Wondered if you'd do me a favor, Boots."

"Sure, even if you are a Yankee."

The war was still with us. Boots was all Louisiana and I was all Kansas. The part of Kansas that had stayed blue.

"You hear what happened to Starcrossed?"

He was a solid, somewhat stolid man. Easygoing. But when I mentioned Starcrossed, he reacted more than usual. His head jolted backward. Starcrossed was the main draw of the race.

"Yeah. Shitty thing to happen." He dusted his chaps off and then did the same with his shirt. He'd gotten dusty in the corral. "What's Jake say?"

"Not too much. Nobody's saying much. But everybody's a little spooked."

His face tightened. "Hell, Dev. Could be just some kind of natural thing he was goin' through. Or —"

"Or somebody put something in his feed."

He nodded.

"I've got to ask you something you probably won't want to do." I paused. "I'm out here working for the President. Everybody knows that. But I'm also doing some things people don't know about."

I wasn't ready to tell him, or anyone, about Tess O'Neill yet.

"Tell me what it is," he said. He sounded curious. "I'll be the one to decide if I want to do it or not."

"If you hear or see anything suspicious," I said, "would you bring it to me first? Even before Steffens, I mean. You're kind of the

60

leader of the guards. And I'll pay you for it."

"No need for that." He gave me a thin smile. "The pay, I mean. You know how I feel about horses. Like them a whole lot better than I do humans. And anybody who'd try and hurt Starcrossed — I better not catch the prick, if you know what I mean."

"I appreciate this, Boots. I really do."

A cowboy inside the corral called his name.

"Well, I better get back at it." Then he smiled. "Say, there is one thing you could do for me."

"Name it."

"Get me a date with that lady reporter. The one who's always hangin' around the prince. Natalie?"

I grinned, too. "You noticed her, did you?"

"She's all we talk about at night in the bunkhouse."

I told him I'd see what I could do, but both of us knew he didn't have much of a chance.

Amanda was waiting for me as I started walking back toward the track.

"Dad still can't figure out what happened to Starcrossed," she told me. "He's calmed down. But I don't think Dad's telling me everything that's on his mind."

"He's probably just scared something else might happen to the horse. Starcrossed has never done anything like that, and Jake doesn't want to say anything till he's sure of what he's saying."

There was a refreshment stand down near the place where buggies would be parked. It was slightly out of our way but on a skin-boiling day like this — it was already eighty and headed for close to ninety — lemonade sounded good even though it was barely nine-thirty.

We had to wade, wend, and wriggle our way through a couple of hundred kids who'd come out here with various church groups. Steffens was always trying to make people think that racing was still the great American sport, unsullied and a fine pastime for people of all ages, despite fixed races and quite a bit of gambling and violence.

"You know, if I didn't know better, I'd say you were a cowboy." Amanda smiled when we finally got a spot on a picnic bench in the shade of a huge cedar tree. "You even look like you could slap leather if you wanted to with that .44 of yours." She reached across the table and touched my hand. "I wish you weren't such an old fogy so I could marry you."

I enjoyed her chatter, but my enjoyment, on this particular morning, came to a quick halt.

Six

I'd never known anybody who smirked as much as Harry Wilhelm. I'd worked with him briefly during the war blowing up railroad track behind Southern lines. In the first five minutes of our first meeting he'd managed to drop in the supposed facts that he'd graduated Phi Beta Kappa from Harvard and that he was only working as a spy because he thought it would give him material for his first novel, which would be, according to Harry and his smirk, enough to make New York drop to its knees and plead for just a glimpse of this great *artiste*.

The trouble was, as I found out several years after the war, that not a single thing Harry told me about himself had been true. He'd been in prison from the age of sixteen to twenty-three and had never finished grade school. All his book learning had come from the prison library. I got this over tequila one night in a small café on the

Mexican border where the Boss had sent me to negotiate the release of an American ambassador's daughter.

She'd been kidnapped while trying to talk a gang of Mexican bandits into going back to church and walking the righteous path to eternal salvation. She was a missionary, but well intentioned as those folks are, they can be awfully damned naïve and cause a lot of mighty sticky problems for their governments. But the Boss was a good friend of the ambassador's and had in fact been at the christening of this young woman. Which is how I got involved in the mess, in spite of my misgivings.

The man whom the Boss had assigned to deliver the ransom money turned out to be Harry Wilhelm's brother Leonard, who wasn't nearly as much fun as Harry and all his colorful smirky bullshit stories, but who was one hell of a lot more honest. Harry had offered his younger brother to the Boss in return for the Boss's convincing a federal judge that Leonard would be much more valuable to his country (the Boss can get awfully dramatic) than sitting in a jail cell. So the Boss hired Leonard, but showed his contempt for the kid by giving him every suicide job he could find.

Leonard was to deliver the ransom money

to our *bandido* friends, which explains how Leonard and I came to be drinking together the night before the money drop. And which also explains how I came to learn Harry Wilhelm's real story.

The kid didn't have any luck with the *bandidos.* Two days after he went into the mountains with the money, his *cojones* were mailed back to the local sheriff along with a photograph of a cowering and very naked young woman. There was a scrawled note on the back indicating that poor Leonard was dead and that the girl was being gang-raped every day. Now they had the money and the girl.

And then Harry Wilhelm showed up. He'd been working close by on a counterfeit conspiracy. I didn't realize how much he cared about his little brother until after we rounded up as mercenary a posse as we could find and went into the mountains and dealt with the *bandidos* ourselves.

I kept thinking about what the girl had gone through. It made it easier to shoot four of them in the back as they warmed their hands over a campfire. Harry rounded up the other three and then gut-shot them all, insuring a lingering and horrible death. It would be a race between them dying of blood loss or getting eaten alive by coyotes.

As he shot them, tears streamed down his cheeks and he kept saying, over and over, in a voice that hinted at madness, "He was just a kid, you bastards. Just a kid."

Harry and I had parted company after that, as the Boss didn't want him on the payroll any longer. The Boss had some angry words for me, too, but since I'd brought the ambassador's daughter back alive, if not unsoiled, he was willing to forgive me. What Harry had done, however, was a little raw for even the Boss to swallow.

Now, three years later, in the scorching sun, intruding on the lemonades Amanda and I were sharing, Harry Wilhelm came into view.

He stood to the left of our little picnic table and said, "Well, I'll be damned. Dev Mallory."

He was smirking, of course, when he said it.

Even at twenty pounds overweight, Harry managed to keep his attraction for women. He had the kind of male theatricality that even smart women often mistake for charm. The bow, the hand-kissing, the grand goodbyes. Somehow Harry made all his bullshit work.

"My Lord, Dev," he said, touching his

large hands to the vest of his suit, "is this your daughter? I don't believe I've ever seen a creature more beautiful."

I was disappointed to see how quickly a smile came to Amanda's face. I had hoped she'd be more sensible than that. But the force of this one-man stage show had great power — until you'd seen it in action too many dreary times, as most of us Boss-slaves had.

He came over and took her hand and kissed it with great charm and reverence, and then looked over at me and said, "No offense, Dev, but I wouldn't have thought you could have produced a child this lovely. Her mother must really be a beauty."

Amanda giggled, actually giggled. "Why, I'm not his daughter."

I said, sour as I could make it, "Amanda, meet the great Harry Wilhelm. He knows you're not my daughter. He just wants to make a good entrance." I nodded to the pose he'd struck. "And you can let go of her hand now, Harry."

"You're enchanting, my dear. You truly are."

He gave her digits another brush of his full lips and then returned said digits to their rightful owner.

"We don't see enough of each other, Dev.

Since I left the Boss in Washington, I doubt I've seen you twice. And I left three years ago."

In that time, according to the stories I'd heard of his exploits, Harry had been arrested for such crimes as mail fraud, bank robbery, extortion, and arson. Note that I said *arrested*. Not *convicted*. When he took the witness stand in his own behalf, Harry went into the sad story of his life, none of which was true, of course, but it made for a five-hankie performance. Had anybody ever been as abused as Harry Wilhelm? Not that you'd ever heard of. And yet poor Harry had been able to rise above his vile origins, at least as he told it. He then went all patriotic on them, and Harry as a patriot is enough to make even the upper classes sick. Harry spoke of the battles and narrow escapes and death-defying espionage work he'd had to endure as a spy and intelligence agent for his country. More hankies, please. Not guilty on every charge.

"Nice to see you're drinking lemonade, my friend," Harry said, the smirk on prominent display. "Poor old Dev here was treated very badly by his former wife, and there were a few years there where old Dev would get very drunk and very nasty. We all tried to help him through it."

69

"What can I do for you, Harry?"

"Nothing. Nothing at all, Dev. I'm just here to place a few bets and enjoy the race. And say hello to Carter Steffens. He's an old friend."

"He's no doubt a Harvard man," I said, "just like you."

He didn't respond at all. He turned, lifted Amanda's hand to his lips, kissed it, and then returned it to her with great care. "I hope I see you again, my dear. You're too lovely to bid *adieu*."

Thirty seconds later, he was part of the growing crowd, invisible. I hoped he'd stay that way, but somehow I doubted it would work out like that.

Amanda watched him until he disappeared from our sight. "I don't think I've ever met anybody like him."

"Then you're lucky."

"You looked like you wanted to kill him. And he looked the same way about you." She paused. "And you never told me you were married."

I shrugged. "Long ago and far away, young lady. And I'm finally over it. At least I hope so."

"Sounds like she really cheated on you."

I nodded. "Yep. She really did."

But she wasn't really interested in me and

70

my sad story. She was still thinking of God's greatest gift to the stage. "By the way, what does *adieu* mean?"

"It means good-bye. And that's what I have to say right now."

"Gee, it sounds so — I don't know — so kind of fancy when Harry says it."

What a romantic kid.

"Yeah," I said. "Good old Harry."

I stopped at the track on my way to the backstretch. I wondered if Jake had figured anything out about Starcrossed yet.

Steffens was in the infield with two men who puffed on big cigars and managed to look imperious even from this distance. Didn't Steffens ever get sick of kowtowing to people, of doing all their ridiculous bidding? He was rich, but he acted like a servant around anybody he deemed important. After the war I spent some time living in Washington. That's how they run it there. A handful of men with power make everybody else bow and scrape. I didn't last long there. I get a sharp pain in my back, not to mention other places, when I have to bow.

I'd been lucky to squeeze into a place at the fence. So-called "railbirds" crowded it, not to watch the horses or the jockeys, but to experience the great thrill of seeing the inner rail being painted an even more brilliant white.

That had no appeal to me. I wanted to get a look at some of Starcrossed's competitors. I hadn't had time for paying attention to anything except security and making an effort to identify all the known grifters.

Exciting as it was watching that fence being painted, I pushed on to the stables. Time to check on them again. By now I'd gotten to know most of the trainers and their staffs by look if not by name. Everybody nodded and hurried on to their work.

There is nothing quite as invigorating as the various scents of a stable. You've got your horseshit, your hay, your earthen floor, your various horse medicines, and your horse odor. It wasn't as heady as a whorehouse, but it had its points.

The frenzy was bad in there. Stalls were packed with trainers, owners, jockeys. Lesser folk ran in and out of the stables on numerous missions.

Horse people, from the elite jumpers of high society to the racetrack crazies who walk around mumbling to themselves, are personally willing to surrender their dignity, their money, and sometimes their lives to an animal that is not, strictly speaking, among the smartest walking the planet.

Today there were a lot of cowboys, too, horse ranchers down from the surrounding hills, enlisted to add some kind of local knowledge to the training procedures. That was their somewhat obscure explanation for hanging around the stables. My own feeling was that Steffens had them here to keep local folks involved and thereby keep them happy.

And supposedly all of these people, as oddly assorted a bunch as you were ever likely to see in one place, had been approved by Steffens. And all of them had the identifying ribbon and card. I could see now that trying to keep track of everyone was hopeless. Anyone with a minimum of criminal skill could fake the ribbon and forge the card. But at least we were trying to keep the riffraff out.

Amanda stood next to the prince, her hip touching his. Even from the back they made a good-looking couple. Some pairs of men and women just look right. You can't even explain it. Just the right proportions, posture, hair color. Amanda and John looked that way to me. Too bad the prince himself didn't see it.

Jake had a currycomb, running it over Starcrossed's neck. The animal sure looked peaceful now. No one would ever have guessed that only a few hours before he'd been wilder than a shit-house rat.

"You figure anything out yet?" I asked Jake.

All three of them turned to look at me.

Jake shrugged. "All we can hope was that it was some kind of temporary abnormality. I checked out his water and his food and couldn't see or smell anything that looked funny in there. I'm not a doc or a scientist, but I've seen plenty of tricked-up food before. Didn't see anything close to that today."

I believed him, but I wasn't ready to rule anything out, not even something added to the food or water. The fact that Jake couldn't smell it didn't mean it wasn't there.

"All the time I've had Starcrossed," John said, "he's never done anything like this morning. He's given me less trouble than any horse I've ever owned." He smiled at Amanda. "I can remember this young lady telling me that Starcrossed didn't seem aggressive enough to compete because he was so gentle and sweet."

"I sure learned I was wrong," Amanda said, smiling back at the prince.

There didn't seem much reason for me to stay around here so I said good-bye.

SEVEN

A couple of times, I thought I saw Tess O'Neill. She was on my mind more than I realized. I'd feel this jolt in my chest, like somebody had hit me there pretty hard, but then it would go away as soon as I realized that it wasn't Tess at all.

I was trying not to think of all the things they might be doing to her. She might even be dead by now. I'd also realized that she might not have touched my flask at all. Maybe they'd managed to get her out of the train car at knife- or gunpoint.

And why had they moved her? Had they gotten someone else to agree to poison Starcrossed? Maybe they'd realized that I would never do it, not even to save Tess.

And Tess knew it. Anybody who signed on to work for the Boss, even if she was on loan from the Secret Service, knew the risks involved and was willing to accept them.

To tell the truth, I was probably worrying

far too much. Tess was tough, and she was smart. If anybody could survive a kidnapping, she was the one. Or so I kept telling myself. I just wished that Harry hadn't turned up. Seeing him had reminded me of the kidnapping of the ambassador's daughter, and things certainly hadn't turned out well that time.

That time, however, the kidnappers hadn't been dealing with Tess. She was equipped to handle them if they gave her half a chance. And if they gave her half a chance, they were going to be mighty surprised.

I hadn't heard from the Boss. Usually when he gets bad news, he fires off a telegram telling me what an incompetent I am. But he hadn't responded to my news about Tess at all. Maybe he was too pissed off to even write a telegram.

A gaunt man in a dark suit appeared in front of me suddenly. "I would to excuse me, but the Lady Hawes would to speak to you." He seemed flustered by the fact that he couldn't speak English very well. "I am usually the manservant, and I do not have to speak to much strangers."

He smiled and shook his head.

I shrugged my response, not knowing exactly how to respond.

"To follow, please."

I understood that well enough. He took off, and I trailed along behind him. We ended up back in the parking area behind the grandstand. The wagons of suppliers outnumbered the private buggies and surreys now.

They sat in a hansom cab. A man who could have been the twin of the manservant sat up top, holding the reins of a mare.

Elizabeth Hawes didn't get out of the cab, simply addressed me through the door she'd swung open. Her mother sat next to her, staring straight ahead. Apparently she didn't want to sully her eyes on a commoner.

"Thank you for seeing me."

"Sure. What can I do for you?"

"I would like you to set up an appointment for me."

"An appointment?"

"The girl, the daughter of the trainer." The disdain was strong in her tone. I tried not to be damaged by her beauty, but it was impossible. There should have been a flaw somewhere on the face or the body presently sheathed in a white linen summer dress. But none was to be seen. There was even a hint of nipple, the left nipple if you want all the facts, pressed against the linen of the dress. This would probably be fine in Europe, but out here the descendants of the people who ran the witch trials were constantly on the prowl even now. Not that I was one of them. I knew how to appreciate what I was trying hard not to stare at.

"I want to tell her the truth about John."

The mother finally turned slightly to look at me. "We're doing this for her sake."

"Yes, for her sake," Liz Hawes said. "So he does not hurt her. He has hurt many women."

"Many, many women," added her mother, fleshy in a dress much like her daughter's.

"He also drinks more than he should."

"And gambles."

This was getting amusing, but I tried not to smile.

"And yet you want to marry him," I said.

Liz started to say something in reply, but her mother interrupted. "She is considering it only because she can save him from his ways. She is his true love."

"The only true love he's ever had," I said.

"Yes," Liz said without any irony that I could detect.

"Even," the mother added, "if he doesn't realize it yet."

"Well, I can't speak for Amanda."

I wanted to work her name into the conversation. They obviously didn't want to speak it.

"But you could arrange it," the mother said with a crafty azure eye. "We're told you're a man who can arrange things. A ruffian, but something of a diplomat. Mr. Steffens himself told us that."

" 'A ruffian, but something of a diplomat.' That's almost a compliment."

"This is very serious business, Mr. Mallory," Liz said. "You should not smile in this manner." An accent here, too.

"What if she won't agree with it?"

"You'll convince her to agree with it," Mother said.

"I wish I was as powerful as you seem to think I am. But people don't do things just because I ask them to."

"Don't ask her," Mother said, "tell her."

"I see. And if she doesn't do it, I slap her around a little."

"I've warned you about the humor," Liz said. "It is not appropriate here."

They were a lot of fun, these two. Why Prince John wouldn't want to spend the rest of his young life with them was beyond me. Hell, for all I knew, maybe he did.

"Well, I'll do what I can."

Liz leaned forward. A roundness of pale breast peeked above the top of her low-cut dress. She was beautiful in a way that was not quite human. Falling in love with her would be like falling in love with a statue in a museum. You could never possess her in any messy way that involved lust or sentimental attachment. And if you tried, Mother would be there to slap you over the head three or four times.

"And please be sure to emphasize that this is all for her sake," Mother said. "If she doesn't wish to talk to us, which I suppose is possible, perhaps you can carry our message for us. You can tell her what the prince is really like."

"I just met him."

"You can mention that he has spells," Liz said.

"Spells?"

"Yes. There are times when he's quite mad. I found him in a forest one day talking to jays and squirrels and deer. He seemed to be under the impression that they understood him."

"Maybe they did."

"Your humor again, Mr. Mallory." This time it was mother rather than daughter who chided me about my jokes.

"I'll try and do something about that for you. Maybe there's a surgical way to have it removed. Like tonsils. Or warts."

"We'll expect to hear from you forthwith," huffed Mother. Daughter slammed the door hard enough to shake the entire cab.

The driver, top-hatted and tailed, surprised me by looking down from his perch and winking at me and then shaking his head.

Good to know it wasn't just me who found them about as irritating as any two people I'd ever met.

After leaving the two women, I made a swing through the grounds. The day was heating up fast. I spent what was left of the morning, which wasn't much, writing up a report to send to the Boss, and then I headed for the picnic area where the ranch hands took most of their meals.

Ham, beans, big slices of wheat bread, and narrow slices of blueberry pie made for fine dining for somebody of simple tastes like me. Fancy cuisine sounds better in theory than it tastes in reality.

The boys' conversation was usually divided between bitching about Steffens and sharing the latest "naughty" jokes. The really dirty ones had to be saved for later because Amanda had joined us. "Naughty" was okay with her, but downright "dirty" was something else.

After about a half hour the boys drifted back to the corral. The press had requested an interview with the boys, and Steffens, understandably, was only too happy to oblige.

Amanda and I talked a bit about Star-crossed, but she had no further information to offer, other than the fact that John seemed to her to be somewhat more upset than he'd let on.

I debated telling her about my conversation with Liz Hawes, but I decided against it. This wasn't the right time. Amanda had enough on her mind without my adding to it. So I told her good-bye and went to my quarters.

Quarters was a military tent that contained a cot and a lot of blankets that were useless in the heat. The musty smell of hot canvas reminded me for a moment of all the tents I'd occupied during the war and of other things I'd rather not have remembered. But I was cheered by the fact that nobody had shown up to share the tent. There's a kind of loneliness I like, and not having some talky bastard as a tent partner is one of them.

One thing I liked about being alone was that I could read if I wanted to, with nobody to criticize my choice of books. The kind of thing I read more often than not was some cheap yellowback. I once tried to convince a lady I wanted to impress that the only novels I read were by Nathaniel Hawthorne. But then we shared a hotel bed for two nights during which she found my supply of yellowbacks. She laughed and said I should be ashamed of myself.

That night as a joke, when the fun was over and we were each reading by lamplight, she said, "I bought you something today." At which point she handed me a copy of *The Scarlet Letter.* You read about these magic sleeping powders. They have nothing on old Nate, let me assure you. Two pages and I was in deep slumber. I never did get any farther than that in the book, and in fact I'd left it behind in the hotel. I hoped that some sleepless traveler had found it useful.

I smiled as I remembered. I wondered if I should buy another of Hawthorne's novels and give it a try. But I didn't wonder long. I stretched out on the cot, and pulled a yellowback out from underneath it. This time our hero was fighting a gang of Chinese bank robbers. Disguised as an elderly Chinese man, our hero was presently overhearing a conversation in an opium den. Would our hero be forced to smoke opium? Was America ready for a drugged Master of Disguise?

A voice from outside said: "Are you in there, Mr. Mallory?"

"Yes. Who is it?"

"Marshal Rossiter."

"C'mon in."

I'd been trying to meet Rossiter since I reached town. I was told he was in another county testifying at a trial.

He was a tall, slim man with an angular face, a white Vandyke beard, and a dusty black suit. He made no effort to hide the Frontier Colt slung across his midsection. You might mistake him for a businessman until you saw the gun and the eyes. There was a lot of cold anger in those dark eyes. I wondered if the anger had anything to do with the somewhat crabbed way he walked. He walked at a slight angle, favoring his right hip.

I stood up and offered my hand.

We shook and I said, "Let's sit outside. This tent's heating up."

"Good idea. We get a lot of sun here. That's supposed to help my rheumatism. Damned stuff nearly cripples me sometimes."

Outside, we sat on a couple of crates under a shade tree.

"I just stopped by to say that I've been

informed about why you're here and that I'd like to cooperate with you, Mr. Mallory."

"Dev'll do fine."

"And call me Paul."

"Well, that's what I'm hoping for, too. Co-operation. A lot of lawmen resent federal people, and I don't blame them. Some people get that federal tag on them, and they think they run the world."

He nodded. "That's been my experience. That's why I wanted to meet and see if we couldn't hash out any problems right from the git-go."

"I'm here to make sure that the prince and his horse are protected properly. I'm also supposed to look out for any grifters who've been involved in major crimes."

He smiled for the first time. Even the eyes suggested a certain amusement. "Meaning I get the purse snatchers and the pickpockets."

"There's going to be a lot of money — millions, I expect — won and lost on this race. Every major confidence man in the country is out here. The smart ones are running the kind of con I'm not smart enough to detect. They won't try for the big jackpot, just a nice plump small one. The ones who go for the big jackpot, I'll be able to spot. There'll be plenty for both of us to do."

"How about the ones that would try to hurt Starcrossed?"

"Well, that's the most obvious approach. I've heard a lot about that kind of thing around the country. Just in the last year, there was a groom who drugged a horse. There have been jockeys who used illegal prods; jockeys who slowed their horses down so another horse would win. At one place back East there was a new twist. Instead of drugging the horse, they drugged the jockey."

"And that's all possible here?"

I laughed. "I'm sure there's that and a lot more I don't know about. At this level of crook, the crooks are smarter than we are more times than we like to admit."

"Which is the easiest con to uncover?"

"Doping the horse, I suppose. A good vet can do a blood check and spot it pretty easily."

"What about a bad vet?"

"You're catching on. Last year in New York, a bad vet got a lot of money to say that he couldn't find any drugs in the winner's blood. But the racing commission kept pushing and finally got an honest vet in there. He found plenty of dope in the blood."

"You're going to be a busy man, Dev."

"I'm afraid I am."

Rossiter looked around the milling crowd. "This is the biggest event in the history of this place. I'd be working the crowds myself, but walking isn't so easy for me anymore."

"Yeah, I guess I noticed that."

"Sure you noticed it. Everybody does. They pretend not to. Cripples embarrass people. People feel sorry for them. And one thing I've learned is that after a while, folks start to dislike people they have to feel sorry for. It becomes a burden. You can't have a nice, normal conversation because you have to be careful around a cripple — same as you do around a Mexican or a colored man — you don't want to say the wrong thing and hurt his feelings. And you get tired of that after a while. So you start avoiding the cripple."

"Seems like they didn't get real tired of you. They voted you back in."

The smile showed some bitterness. "I told my wife this is my 'pity term.' They figure they owe me something for getting shot six different times. They're good people, this town. But next year there'll be another election and they'll want a more regular guy." He tapped his right hip. "One who can get up and run if he has to. My wife says it goes to show you that you try and do somebody a nice turn and look what happens."

He splayed his hands over his knees and levered himself up and said, "Sorry for all the talk."

"Hell, I enjoyed it."

He gave me a long stare. He was likely listening for any hint of scorn in my voice.

Then: "Well, I'm looking forward to working with you."

"Same here, Paul."

I went back into my tent and lay on the cot again and picked up my yellowback book. Our hero was apparently a celibate. There were never any girls around.

The serious trouble started that night.

A fire horn rousted us from our seats and pushed us to the door. Few things are scarier than a blaze in the area of a stable, not only because of the danger to the horses but because of the danger to the men trying to save them. The fire is bad enough. Frightened horses make it much worse. In their panic, they pay no attention to whoever might be nearby, and they're as likely to kill the one trying to help them as not.

Because the racetrack workers were so skilled at dealing with emergencies, the fire was limited to a single wing of the intricate design of the stables.

The fury of the fire was ferocious enough to spook all the other animals in even safe parts of the building. They screamed like terrified children. I could hear them kicking the wooden doors of their stalls. A crowd of maybe one hundred men had already formed a semicircle, watching, hoping that the horses could be saved. Their bodies were bronzed with the color of the flames. There was a lot of coughing. The smoke was heavy.

"I'm worried that Dad is in there," Amanda said, rushing up to me. "I haven't seen him all evening. Do something, Dev!"

I was worried about Jake, too.

"Where the hell's Jake?" I shouted at one of the nearby track officials.

He was watching the men who'd been trained to deal with fires. They were damned efficient. The heat from the flames pushed us back, nearly blistering our skin.

"How the hell would I know where he is, Mallory? I'm worried about Starcrossed. Jake can take care of himself."

"You bastard!" Amanda shouted back at him, her words lost in the crackling insanity of a fire that was spreading fast. The fact that her father might well be in this wing of the stables had made her crazy.

"Wait here," I said.

She started to argue — she wasn't the

kind of woman who stayed behind when her father was in trouble, no matter what the danger to herself — but I walked away quickly, winding my way in and out of small groups of folks fascinated by the flames.

The next three people I asked gave me pretty much the same answer. The horses were what mattered, not Jake.

I was about to start swinging at the next track official I spotted when a large and undeniable hand clamped my shoulder.

"Get the hell away from here, Mallory, and stop bothering my people!"

Carter Steffens held me in his powerful grip and turned me so that I was facing him.

"I have to find Jake!" I shouted into the increasing *whoosh* of flame and the yelling of the crowd.

"Right now, I'm more worried about Starcrossed. Jake'll be fine."

I turned to face the fire. Tried to hear if there were any human screams. All the clamor made that impossible. I worried about Amanda being alone. If Jake was found dead, I wanted to be with her. For all her appealing beauty, she was one of those loners you suspect are facing down some private dreads that keep them from making any real friends. Maybe that was why the prince hadn't fallen for her. That didn't matter now, though. I wanted to help her. If Jake died, there'd be nothing left for her. I doubted that even her relationship with Starcrossed would be much consolation.

I jerked my shoulder away from Steffens and stalked away for a better look at the far side of the stable wing that was on fire.

The smoke was getting worse, coming now in rolling ghostlike billows that made it difficult to see if there was any way into the building from this angle.

Not only would there be no way out — there was no way in. Even if I rushed in now, the smoke would take me down before I had any hope of finding Jake. And nobody was sure yet where he was. Hardly anyone seemed even to care.

I kept moving, looking for another possible way in.

Just as I sighted the open back door — a black rectangle in the red-gold flame — the great cosmic hand of Carter Steffens was on me again. "Forget about it, Mallory. The President's a friend of mine. If I let you go in there, he'd kick my ass from here to Hawaii. You're the man he put in charge of guarding the prince and his horse. You know your job. And you're damned well going to do it."

But right then I didn't give a damn about

my job or the Boss or anything except finding Jake. Right in the middle of Steffens's little speech, I wrenched myself free of his godlike grip and started running for the back door of the stable.

But you didn't go against Carter Steffens's wishes. He came right after me. Bellowing for me to stop, his glory days as a football player back East apparently coming back to him in terms of energy and skill, he caught up with me.

I was ten feet from the doorway — Steffens was still coming after me — when it happened. I didn't hear it happen; still too much noise for that. I'm not sure I even felt it happen, at least not at the time I usually would.

Something pushed me backward, something as powerful as the kick of a horse. But there were no horses nearby. I'd been shot.

Shot at the exact moment Carter Steffens was playing football again, tackling me and bringing me down with such force that my forehead hit the unyielding ground at a pretty good rate of speed. I was unconscious instantly.

EIGHT

It was much later when I finally got back to the bunkhouse that night. I was weak and tired and thinking maybe I should have taken the doc up on his offer of a cot for the night.

I'd been taken to the doctor in Steffens's buggy, and I parked it near the stables so I could check in there. I wanted to see how Starcrossed was doing.

Before going to the doc's, I'd come to enough to put Boots Donovan in charge.

"You're up and around already?" he asked.

"The wound isn't bad. Just kind of grazed me." I smiled. "Took out a little chunk of my left shoulder, but the doc says I'll be fine."

And he was probably right. Still, my shoulder hurt like hell, and I itched under the bandage.

"Who the hell would want to shoot you?"

It was a damned good question. Too bad I

didn't know the answer. I didn't know why, either. Whoever had done it had escaped easily in all the confusion.

"That's an ugly bruise on your forehead."

I thought about Steffens and the tackle he'd laid on me.

"Could have been worse. I'm lucky I have a hard head. You expecting an invasion?"

"Huh?"

The section of the stables where Starcrossed was being kept looked like an armed camp. I'd asked for a pair of guards. Boots had put three of the cowboys and two of the local *gendarmes* on it. Two rifles on the left side of the wing where Starcrossed was now being kept, two on the right side. And Boots.

"Five rifles."

"Oh." He gave me a crooked grin. "I guess it's like that old saying about locking the barn door after somebody's taken the horses, but I thought we'd better be sure there wasn't any more damage." The grin disappeared and his tone turned serious. "I'm sorry as hell about Jake. I guess you heard."

I'd heard, all right. Someone had brought the news to the doc's, and Steffens had left with him right away, which was how I'd

come to be driving the buggy back by myself.

"Anybody know what happened?" I asked.

"Not that I've heard of. Hell, we all thought everything was taken care of. All the horses were okay, but Jake never showed up. They found him in the ashes after they got the fire out."

"Where in the ashes?"

"Not far from where Starcrossed would've been. He must've been trying to get the horse out."

"No way to tell what happened to him?"

"He was burned pretty bad. That's all I know about it."

"How's Starcrossed?"

"Fine. They brought some vet in from town." He shook his head. "Poor old Jake. I sure did love to hear him talk with that funny accent."

Jake's Scottish burr that we wouldn't be hearing again. I guess we'd sounded funny to him, too, or maybe he'd gotten used to us over the years.

"Well, I'm headed to the bunkhouse. I take it you're going to rotate the guards tonight, yourself included?"

"Yeah, that's the plan."

"See you in the morning, then."

I turned to go, but Boots called me back.

"I forgot to tell you. That prince fella stopped by."

"What'd he have to say?"

"He's a funny one. You like him?"

"He's not as much of a pain in the ass as other royalty I've had to work with."

Boots grinned. "Now that sounds like a mighty enthusiastic endorsement. Anyway, he wants to see you in the morning."

I'd been hoping to sleep in, get a few hours of extra rest. Now it looked as if that wasn't a likely possibility.

"Thanks," I said. "I'll handle it."

I started walking toward the bunkhouse again. I stopped for a look at the burned wing of the stables.

The smell was pretty bad — hay, horseshit, wood all up in flame and smoke. All of it had been wetted down pretty well, which added to the stink. In the moonlight the charred remains stood there as a bleak reminder of how out of hand this entire race had gotten.

I knew what was coming. Starting tomorrow there would be protests against the presence of the prince in this town. There would be a group protesting the fact that this race was rigged and that the governor should cancel it — an antigambling group that was gathering as much momentum as the antialcohol groups around the country, both focusing on how gambling and liquor destroyed families. They weren't unreasonable causes, and I could even sympathize with them, but I didn't see that they'd amount to much in the long run. Human beings are drawn to certain types of self-destruction. Maybe we believe that deep down we deserve it. Don't know any other creature that does this. Next time you see a pair of raccoons playing blackjack, let me know.

The bunkhouse door was open and judging by the light streaming through the windows, all the lanterns were lit. That wasn't right. Cowboys at the end of a cattle drive liked to drink and carouse all night. Cowboys who had to work early, as these gents did, went to bed damned early, especially after a hard night like the one they'd had.

Then I heard somebody crying. A man. He'd start to cry, then stop, then start to cry again.

Then there was another sound — one that I was all too familiar with, bone on bone.

Somebody had just hit somebody real hard in the face.

I had just walked through the door when another punch was delivered.

A cowboy named Briney was lashed to a chair. His face was puffy and bloody from punches.

Another cowboy named Rand stood over him. He wore a tan leather glove on his right hand. The glove was bloody.

Two racetrack employees stood off to the side watching the beating.

"Goddamnit," I said. "What the hell's going on here?"

NINE

It took a few minutes to get the story straight, but it seemed that the two racetrack employees had seen a man running away from the wing of the stables that had been burned down tonight. The two men hadn't managed to get a good look at him, but they noticed that he ran with a slight limp.

They saw him again about twenty minutes later, his clothes changed, trying to mingle with the crowd that was watching the fire. They knew him by the limp. This time they got a good look at him. It was Chip Briney.

He saw that they were onto him and took off again. He didn't try to outrun them. He did what he had the first time they spotted him. He hid out, hoping that they hadn't seen his face.

They couldn't find him at first, but they figured that he was somewhere on the grounds with one of the six or seven groups of cowboys who were going to participate in the rodeo that Steffens planned to put on the morning of the race.

They found him in the bunkhouse, pretending to sleep. Rand and his two friends came in while the track employees were interviewing him. Rand had scoffed at the way they were handling Briney. He said that if Briney had started the fire, he deserved to be questioned in a way that would get the truth out of him the fastest way possible, and the two track employees had told him to go to it.

Rand had just finished beating a partial confession out of Briney before I got there. However, although Briney had confessed to starting the fire, he wouldn't say why he'd done it. Or if anybody else was involved.

I said, "Clean him up."

"You don't give me no orders, federal man."

Rand was excited by what he'd done, beating a man tied to a chair, and he was showing off for the other cowboys.

I decided to do a little showing off of my own. I don't fight to honor the rules. I fight only when it's absolutely necessary, and then I fight to make a point. And when I'm injured and hurting, I'm not about to take any chances with some smart-mouthed bully.

I put my hand into my pocket and slipped on my brass knuckles.

"Hey," Rand said when I brought my hand out.

He wore a black leather vest with a red shirt and a low-slung gun against a pair of black jeans, an outfit calculated to make people afraid of him. He was apparently trying to give the impression that he was a gunfighter. But that breed of man had been killed off nearly a decade back. All that was left were the loudmouths and the bullies.

"I told you to clean him up."

"Get somebody else." He was sullen. He stared straight at the knucks. "You don't try and pull that shit on me."

So that was what I did, of course. I pulled that shit on him and he went down immediately, straight down into a heap. He didn't even have time to groan. I put the knucks back into my pocket.

"Get me some hot water and that medical kit over there."

The other men decided there was no point pissing me off anymore. We'd gotten along fine thus far. They were getting paid well and there was no point jeopardizing it. One of the men took it upon himself to untie Briney without me even asking. Another dragged Rand over to a bunk and pitched him on it.

The man who untied Briney said, "I sure don't know why you went and done a thing like that, Chip. They're going to go rough on you, old son. Real rough."

Briney didn't say anything. He was still kind of stunned.

I got him cleaned up as much as I could. The iodine smarted enough to revive him.

"How you doing, kid?" I said.

"He really beat on me, Mr. Mallory."

His words were slurred, and I figured he had some loose teeth to go with his split lips and mangled face.

"I know he did. But how about you? Did you set that fire?"

He raised his head. The lantern light gleamed on the lumps, bumps, bruises, and blood knots on his face. He gaped around at the others.

"You boys go get some beer somewhere," I said. "Get a little air. I need half an hour here."

"He done it," one of the track workers said. "He damned well done it. He said so, and we all heard him. Ain't that right, boys?"

They all agreed that he had.

"So don't you let him say otherwise," the man said.

"Thanks for the advice. Now clear out."

They left, except for Rand, who was snoring lightly on the bunk. He was in no condition to go anywhere. Not that it mattered, since he was also in no condition to hear what was said or to interfere.

Briney sat slumped in the chair. No energy, all pain.

I sat on one of the single beds facing him. He didn't raise his head to try to look at me.

"Setting that fire wasn't your idea," I said.

He didn't answer.

"You might as well tell me, Chip. Maybe I can help you. So was it your idea or not?"

He hesitated a second, then said, "No, sir, it wasn't."

"Whose was it then?"

He looked sad and without warning started to cry a little. "I wish I could tell ya."

I looked over at Rand.

"You don't want to go through all this bullshit again, do you?"

"You gonna hit me?"

"No. But I'll be damned tempted to if you don't start talking."

"I give my sacred word."

He wasn't old enough to grow a mustache, but he was trying hard. He looked so young and sounded so scared. He'd been an easy mark for somebody.

"You get paid to do it?"

"No, sir."

"Nothing at all?"

"No, sir."

"There wasn't anything in it for you?"

"I can't answer that, sir. Like I said, I give my sacred word."

"A man died in that fire," I said. "A damned good man."

He cried a little more, then snuffled and said, "I know that. It wasn't supposed to be that way."

It was a line I'd heard all too many times. The people like Chip, the young and scared ones, never meant to hurt anybody by what they'd done. They'd go back and change it if they could, but it was far too late for that, far too late for Jake Duncan, for Amanda. And for Chip Briney.

"You know you're going to prison, don't you?"

"Yessir." More snuffling.

"Doesn't that scare you?"

"Yessir."

"If you told somebody the truth — if you told who put you up to it — the district attorney might make a deal with you so you wouldn't have to go."

"What's a district attorney?"

I was trying to remember his background. "You from Oregon?"

"Wyoming."

"They have county attorneys there?"

"Yessir."

"Well, it's just about the same thing, county attorney and district attorney."

"They got a real mean one where I come from. He liked to hang a friend of mine, and my friend didn't even do nothin'."

"But you did something. You set a fire, and a man died."

"Nobody intended for that; they really didn't."

No, I thought. But they intended for a lot of animals to die. Or maybe only one. But that was bad enough.

"It doesn't matter what you intended. What happened is all that counts. And here's another thing. Somebody shot me."

Chip looked surprised. "Shot you? You don't look like you've been shot."

"Trust me. The bandages are under my shirt. Did you shoot me, Chip?"

"No, sir. I started the fire, and I'll own up to it, but I sure didn't shoot you. There wasn't to be any shooting involved. That's what I was told."

"Who told you?"

He opened his mouth, and I thought for

part of a second that he was going to tell me. Then he actually grinned.

"You almost tricked me that time, Mr. Mallory. But I don't know who shot you, and I'm not going to tell you anything else. I gave my sacred word."

I was tired of that "sacred word" business, and I wanted to wipe the grin off his face. I took out my makings and rolled a cigarette. After I'd lit it and taken a few puffs, I said, "You remember that district attorney I mentioned?"

"Yes, sir."

"He's going to push for you to be hanged."

That got rid of the grin, all right.

"Nobody intended for nobody to die. And nobody was supposed to get shot."

His bruised cheeks glistened with new, silent tears washing over them.

"The district attorney won't give a good goddamn for that. He'll tell the jury what you did, and then they'll hang you."

Briney gulped and looked lonesome and jittery. His eyes scanned the bunkhouse but found nothing to console him.

"I just can't go back on my sacred word. I just can't."

He started crying harder.

"That man who died tonight," I said. "He was a friend of mine."

But I doubted he heard me. He was lost in his own grief and terror.

TEN

Marshal Rossiter was waiting outside for me when I brought the kid out into the moonlight. The cowboys had drifted away, either to have a beer somewhere or to sleep in another bunkhouse. There wasn't anybody else around. The horses were still noisy down at the stables. Horses can stay spooked for quite a while. And nothing spooks them like a fire.

Rossiter wore the same dusty black suit and the same Colt was strapped across his middle. But this time he was smoking a cigar that you could use as a club.

"I've been listening," he said around the cigar.

"Good for you."

I didn't figure he was going to offer me a cigar, so I rolled a cigarette.

"I take it you've never had much experience as a professional law enforcement officer," he said.

I didn't feel like listening to his bullshit. I blew a puff of smoke in his direction.

"Nothing like a small-town marshal would have."

"No need to take a tone like that. You federal men don't do a whole lot of inter- rogation. Not like us local law enforcement folks. This riffraff here —" He scowled in the general direction of Briney. "This should be a twenty-minute job." He took the cigar from his mouth and tamped on it with the tip of his finger. A huge piece of ash fell to the ground. He snorted; it resembled a laugh. "Now I'm not saying that my pre- ferred techniques are what you would call strictly legal. But I can tell you one thing. They *are* strictly effective." He glared at Briney. "You think his face looks bad now, wait till you see it after I get done with it."

"You ain't gonna let him do that, are you, Mr. Mallory?"

I wondered how much of Rossiter's act was for intimidation and how much he'd actually go through with. There were a good number of citizens' groups petitioning the courts for more civilized treatment of prisoners these days. From what I'd been able to tell, most lawmen in towns of any good size had tightened up the old- fashioned methods of getting confessions.

They'd still slap prisoners around pretty good, but the old days of outright beatings — a good share of which ended up in paralysis or death — were waning.

As one too-clever Chamber of Commerce type had said not so long ago to a crowd of reporters, "This is the New Old West. We kept the good parts and got rid of the bad ones."

I hoped Rossiter had heard that particular spiel.

"I could make a good case for the race-track not being within your jurisdiction, Mr. Rossiter."

"You could. But then we'd have to wake Judge Raeburn up, and he's not a man you'd want to get on the bad side of. Especially if you want to see this young fella here get a fair trial."

"You want me to quote you on that?"

He laughed. "Fine with me. Judge Raeburn says pretty much the same thing himself. If you wake him up, it had damn well better be an emergency."

Chip Briney said, "I want a lawyer."

Rossiter was still being jovial. Or pretending to be, anyway. "See what you started here, Mr. Mallory? You made me bring up the judge, and now this one starts talking about a lawyer. Well, son, you'll have a lawyer." He winked at me. "And she's right pretty, too."

"A woman?" Chip said. "A woman lawyer?"

"Lady lawyers are pretty common these days," I told him. "She's probably just as good as any of the men."

"Yeah, but she don't play gin rummy with the judge," Rossiter said, "the way the men lawyers do."

It was ended and Rossiter knew it and the kid knew it and I knew it. Rossiter produced handcuffs, the kid didn't balk, and then they turned away from the bunkhouse.

They left me there to start thinking about Jake again as I stood in the moonlight, the other cowboys coming back from wherever they'd been and going back into the bunkhouse. It was time for sleep.

I left them to it and went back to my tent. I didn't bother to light the lantern. I sat down on the edge of my cot and rolled a cigarette, trying not to think about the pain in my shoulder. Instead I sat there and smoked and thought about everything that had happened that night and tried to make some sense of it.

Chip Briney was guilty of setting the fire and inadvertently — or so I supposed — killing Jake.

But I had the feeling that that was only part of it. He was still hiding somebody because of his "sacred word."

But who?

I thought of looking up Amanda, but decided against it. It was too late, and I was too tired now. The words would be hard enough to say at the best of times, and now they would come even harder. Not that words were much to put against the death of her father.

The *murder* of her father.

ELEVEN

The misty morning sunlight gave the enormous grandstand a golden glow, making it easy to forget the events of the previous night. Easy to imagine the seats filled with elegant spectators, the men in suits, with bowlers and spats; the women in silk suits and dresses, with huge picture hats and gloves that reached their elbows. The eyes of field glasses would sparkle in the sunlight; the scent of expensive perfumes would mix with the scents of tobacco smoke, whiskey, and beer.

There was even a section built onto the inside of the roof, the glassed-in box where track owners, officials, and their very special friends could watch the race. But for all that the box had seated rich and important people of every kind, it had never seated a prince and his entourage before, as it would the day of the race.

There wasn't much of a crowd this morning, mostly racing people, though some had come from the town to watch the horses in training. Others would come during the day, but they'd be disappointed. The horses would be finished and back in the stables.

Starcrossed and the others had been moved to new quarters, and being high-strung, they'd take their time getting used to the differences.

I was standing near the gate watching the chestnut elegance of Starcrossed working out on the track. He seemed a little jittery, but Gilpin wasn't having any particular trouble with him, certainly nothing like what had happened the day before.

I was beginning to relax when I heard somebody behind me say, "I'm sorry about Jake, miss. He was a fine man."

I didn't need to turn because a moment later Amanda Duncan stood next to me. She had the pale freckled red-haired beauty of Celtic women down the ages. She could easily have been a fashionable lady. Nothing in her demeanor or body type suggested the quick strength she showed when working with horses. But this morning her beauty, strength, and speed were lost to tear-dimmed green eyes, a nose red from crying, and hair that hadn't been combed with much care.

The man who had spoken to her moved away. I started to say something, but she said, "Don't talk for a while, all right, Dev? Let's just watch Starcrossed."

And that's just what we did.

The morning air was cool, clean. The pine-packed foothills to the east added a handsome backdrop to the far side of the track. A train ran westward through the pines, adding a smoky texture to the light up there.

When she spoke, she said, "Dad always said God saved the best for last. He really believed that he'd spent his whole life with horses preparing to handle Starcrossed. These last couple months have been the happiest days of his life."

Before coming to the track here, where I'd joined them, they'd spent two months on a ranch up in Northern California, which was where the prince had played at being a cowpoke and where the Boss had sent Jake to watch over Starcrossed.

As it turned out, Jake could have used a little watching-over himself. I felt bad about that, and not a little guilty.

"He said there were three highlights in his life — when he married my mother, when I was born, and when he started handling Starcrossed."

"I guess I never did know what happened to your mother."

"Influenza. It was pretty bad that year. I guess I was pretty sick, too, but I pulled through."

She spoke in a kind of monotone. She was, I suspected, between long, hard cries. That sort of emotion drains you. You need to get your strength up before you can face another cry.

"It should be me out there with Starcrossed," she said. "Not that bastard Sterling."

Amanda's language had been deteriorating for days now. But she had a point. Sterling looked far too smug to suit me as he watched the groom, Gilpin, put Starcrossed through his paces. You might say that Sterling didn't look a bit upset at the way things had turned out.

"I'm twice the trainer Sterling is," Amanda said. "But no one's going to give me a chance to prove it."

Steffens came up on us then, looking horsey as hell in jodhpurs and bowler. To Amanda he was courtly. He tipped his bowler and said, "I had great respect for your father."

She glanced at me before she spoke. Jake had thought that Steffens was a braggart and a bully. Jake, like most of us, was born to be a worker; Steffens was born to be a boss — not by competence but by birth and the family fortune.

"Thank you, Mr. Steffens."

When he turned to me, he lost his courtly ways. "You didn't do a very good job picking your cowboys, Mallory. You didn't sense anything was wrong with that Briney?"

I didn't remind him that the rodeo was his idea and that I hadn't picked the cowboys. That had been the Boss's doing. He'd picked most of the men who worked on the Northern California ranch where the prince had stayed. But not all of them. A lot of them had been there already, and it's possible that Briney was one of those, not that I'd say that to Steffens, not the way I was feeling at the moment.

"He didn't list 'arsonist' on his application. He just put down bank robber and forger."

I was still pissed off about the way he'd tackled me. My head still hurt. Maybe if he hadn't tackled me, I'd be dead now, but I couldn't bring myself to feel grateful.

"I'm glad you find this humorous," Steffens said.

"I always find you humorous, Steffens. Because you're a joke. If you didn't have

Mommy and Daddy's money, you'd be sweeping streets."

There are moments when you're so angry you can't speak. Your brain is paralyzed with pure rage. You might splutter a bit, as he did. You might make big murderous fists, as he did. You might even have a face so red it's almost scarlet, as he did.

But in the end, all you can do, as he did, is turn around and storm off.

Amanda almost smiled. "You need to watch yourself around him, Dev. We make a joke of it, but he really is a friend of the President. And you're a federal man."

"Right now, I don't give a damn."

My own face was turning scarlet, too. In the dawn chill, my cheeks felt hot.

I grabbed her elbows and looked into that finely sketched face, the perfect freckles on the perfect skin stretched just right on the perfect bones. She looked so damned sad.

"What I got so mad about, Amanda, was him hinting that I didn't do a very good job."

"Oh, Dev, c'mon. You're doing a fine job."

I leaned forward and kissed her on the forehead. When I stepped back from her, I said, "The reason I got so mad at him, Amanda, is that I think he's right. I should've had more guards on that end of the stable. I had them spread too far apart. All he had to do was slip by one of them as soon as it was dark and then sneak inside."

"You're wrong, Dev. And please don't ever run yourself down again like that. What happened last night wasn't your fault."

Then I wondered about something. "I'm going to ask Briney more questions this morning when I get to town. Did you ever see him do anything suspicious all the time you were on the ranch with him and the other cowboys?"

"No," she said. "That's why it's so hard to believe he set the fire. He was this very quiet young fella who loved horses almost as much as Dad did. Dad liked him the best of all the cowboys, in fact."

"But," I said to myself more than to her, "he's the one who set the fire last night. It doesn't make sense."

"No," she said, and I could see that she was ready for another round of crying. "No, it doesn't."

I was trying to make up my mind about whether this was the time to tell her about the "invitation" from Liz Hawes and her formidable mother when Richard Caldwell joined us. His eyes were even more watery than usual, and he seemed on the verge of tears. He pulled at his lip and said something about how sorry he was.

I slipped away and left them there. I felt a little guilty about doing that to Amanda, but I'd remembered that the prince wanted to see me. It wouldn't be polite to keep him waiting too long, not that I was bothered by politeness at the moment. I was still too angry about Jake's death to worry much about the prince's feelings.

The prince was set up for the day in an ornate pavilion. Multicolored banners fluttered from the tips of the poles that held up the bright yellow tent. John sat in a comfortable-looking chair at a small table, drinking coffee. Liz and Davinia Hawes were with him. They were watching the cowboys, who were well away from them at the other end of the infield, working on their rodeo stunts.

When I walked under the tent, John said, "Good morning, Mallory. You seem in excellent health for a man who was shot last night."

"I'm fine," I said, and it was pretty much the truth. My shoulder still burned a little, and I still itched under the bandage, but I could move my arm freely. Another day or two, and I wouldn't even remember being shot.

"Your face doesn't look healthy," Liz

Hawes said.

I smiled at her. She didn't smile back.

"The ground out here is harder than my head," I said.

The prince sensed that things were about to go downhill. He said, "Would you like some coffee, Mallory?"

I said that sounded good, and a man brought me a delicate cup and saucer. There was another chair, and I sat down without being asked. No one seemed to mind except Mrs. Hawes, who gave me a frosty glare. I smiled at her and sipped my coffee. It was hot and it burned my mouth, but I didn't let on. I wasn't going to give her the satisfaction.

"Those cowboys are quite good," the prince said. "But I can do some of those tricks. Did you know that, Mallory?"

"So I've heard," I said.

The prince turned around as if looking for something, but he didn't see it. He said, "Bring me my rope, Carrouthers."

The man who'd given me the coffee showed up a couple of seconds later with a well-worn lariat.

John took it and stood up. "Let me show you a few things I learned at the ranch," he said, and went outside the pavilion.

He was wearing his Western gear, and he

looked enough like a real cowboy to be one. As we watched, he started spinning the rope, working it into a fairly sizable loop. The shadow it made on the infield was even larger than the loop itself.

When he was satisfied that the loop was big enough, John began to hop in and out of it. His shadow hopped along with him, so it was as if there were two of him, one real and substantial, working with the real rope, and another, darker image that jumped into and out of the shadow lariat.

After he'd done that for a while, he made the loop rise up to the level of his shoulders, and then it went back down again, as smoothly as it had risen.

I had to admit that he was pretty good. I'd never learned to handle a rope like that during my cowboying days. I was lucky to be able to rope an errant cow and drag her back to the herd. I tried telling myself that I hadn't learned any fancy tricks because I'd been working too hard and hadn't had time, but I couldn't convince myself. The truth was that when it came to handling a lariat, I wasn't as dexterous as John, and I never would be.

"He's quite good, isn't he?" Liz Hawes said. The morning breeze stirred the hair at the nape of her neck.

I took a sip of coffee before I answered. It had cooled off enough to be almost drinkable.

"Yes," I said. "He's good, all right."

But I couldn't help thinking that John was being just a little disrespectful, what with Jake's death having come only hours before.

John got tired of showing off after a while and came back into the tent. He rolled the lariat into a series of loops and gave it to Carrouthers, who took it away somewhere.

"I think we should talk a bit about last night's fire," he said to me, sitting down at the table.

I put my coffee cup and saucer down. "Jake Duncan died. I think that's what we should talk about."

"An unfortunate accident," John said, frowning. "But surely nothing more than that. He was a fine trainer, and it's a tremendous setback to Starcrossed's training, but Sterling can step in."

I didn't give a damn about Starcrossed or his training at the moment. I said, "We have the kid who started the fire. One of the cowboys named Chip Briney. He won't say why he started it, but it seems pretty clear that he's working for someone else."

I thought about Briney's "sacred word" and wondered just who he'd given it to.

"Where is he now?" John asked.

"At the jail. Marshal Rossiter showed up and claimed him."

"I've met Rossiter. An interesting man."

That wasn't the way I'd have put it, but I nodded as if I agreed.

"But if Briney is in jail," John went on, "then we don't actually 'have him,' do we?"

"Not exactly, but Rossiter didn't give me any choice in the matter. I think you and I should pay Briney a visit this morning. I want to be sure he survives Rossiter's hospitality. And maybe you can be more persuasive than I was with Briney. He might be willing to talk to you."

I didn't really believe it, but it was at least worth a try. John was paying his salary. Maybe he'd feel some kind of obligation.

"Very well." John stood up. "I want to have a look at Starcrossed first. I'll meet you back here in a quarter of an hour." He made a little half bow in the direction of Liz and her mother. "If you ladies will please excuse me."

They said they would, of course, and he went away, leaving me there with them. I'd about as soon have been left in a rattlesnake den, so I thought I'd drift away myself and come back in fifteen minutes to meet the prince. But when I started to get out of my chair, Liz Hawes put up a hand to indicate that I'd better stay right where I was. I decided to humor her to find out what she wanted, though I had a feeling I already knew. I settled back in my chair and waited.

After a short pause, Liz said, "Did you speak to the Duncan girl?"

"You mean Amanda?"

"Very well, if you insist. Amanda. Did you speak to her?"

I was surprised that she could bring herself to say the name. I said, "Speak to her about what?"

"You know very well what," Davinia Hawes said, turning toward me. Her eyes were colder than a winter night in the mountains. "About the things we discussed yesterday."

"I haven't had a chance. Her father was killed last night. Or maybe you didn't know that."

"We know that," Liz said. "Naturally. But it's important that you have her speak with us. Or, failing that, you can tell her what she needs to know, yourself."

I wasn't about to repeat what those two had told me about the prince to anyone, much less Amanda. If they wanted to get the poison out of their systems, they'd have to do it themselves. And they'd have to do it without my help.

"John will be back in a few minutes," I said to Liz. "Why don't you recite his character flaws for him? He might appreciate it. It would give him an opportunity to reform before you marry him. That way, you won't have so much work to do when you tie the knot."

Neither of the women so much as smiled. No emotion at all passed across their faces. I might as well have been talking about the weather in the Sandwich Islands for all the effect my words had on them.

Both of them were physically lovely women, but it seemed to me that something inside of them had withered away and died a long time ago. Conscience, maybe, or the ability to feel anything deeply if it didn't affect them directly. Whatever it was, it was a shame they'd lost it.

I didn't have much experience with women from other countries, women of the so-called nobility, but if these two were any example, I was happy that I'd been spared. Give me an open, feeling woman like Amanda Duncan or Tess O'Neill any day.

The thought of Tess made me wince. I wanted to get my hands on Mitch Clarey, but that would have to wait until I tried to find out more from Chip Briney about why he'd set fire to the stables.

Well, I thought I knew the *why* of it. The *who* was what I needed to know.

But I didn't find that out, either. When John and I got to the jail, Chip Briney was already dead.

TWELVE

The jail was an adobe building left over from the days when the Spanish held California. It was old, but it was solid enough to hold the kinds of prisoners that were likely to be incarcerated in Corvair. It would more than serve to hold a youngster like Briney.

We went to the jail in John's little rig, which he insisted on driving himself. When we walked inside, Rossiter was sitting behind his desk, going through a stack of papers. I saw that they were all fliers with information about various wanted men and a few women, the kind who weren't likely to show up in a town like Corvair. I wondered why Rossiter even bothered.

He looked up when we crossed the threshold. The sun was already hot outside, but the jail's thick walls kept it cool, and Rossiter's customary black suit didn't seem out of place.

"I guess you're here to see the prisoner," he said.

"That's right," I said. "I hope he's not hurt any worse than he was when I left him with you last night."

Rossiter pushed himself away from the battered old desk. It had been in the office a lot longer than he had.

"I don't know what you mean by that, Mallory, but I don't think I like it. I'll let it pass this time. Good morning to you, Prince John."

"Simply John will do," the prince said. "Did Briney say any more to you about the fire?"

"Not a thing." Rossiter took a ring of keys out of the top drawer of the desk. They rattled together as he hefted them. "He seems to think he has some kind of obligation to keep his mouth shut."

I knew about that already. I said, "And you didn't try to persuade him otherwise?"

Rossiter jangled the keys and narrowed his eyes. "That's the second time you've implied something I don't like, Mallory. I sure must have made a bad impression on you last night. Let's let you have a look at the boy, and maybe you'll be happier about things."

He stood up and walked to the cell block

door. He put one of the keys in the lock and turned it smoothly. The hinges squealed when he pushed it open.

"They need a little oil," he said. "Briney's right inside."

He went through the door and into the cell block. John and I followed. The light was quite dim, coming in as it did only from the high, narrow windows in each cell.

"As you can see," Rossiter said, "the prisoner's taking his ease."

Rossiter pointed through the heavy bars that fronted the cell. Briney was lying on a cot at the back. The cell was so small that there was barely room for the cot, but it was clean. I'd been in jails that smelled a lot worse.

Rossiter dragged the key to the cell block door back and forth across the bars. The noise echoed up and down the hallway.

"Wake up, Briney," Rossiter said. "You've got visitors."

Briney didn't move. Dust motes floated through the faint light that filtered down from the high window. The light fell across the lower half of Briney's face, and I could see the vivid bruises where Rand had battered him. And I could see that above the band of light, his eyes were open.

Rossiter continued to clang the key across

the bars. John looked at me and said, "He's an awfully sound sleeper, don't you think?"

"He's not asleep," I said, and it must have occurred to Rossiter at about the same time that nobody could sleep that soundly. He found a key on the ring, stuck the key in the lock on the cell door, and turned it. When he went inside, John and I waited in the narrow hall.

Rossiter took a couple of crabbed steps over to the cot and shook Briney's shoulder. Briney's head lolled to the side, his mouth open.

"Shit," Rossiter said.

He shook Briney again, but Briney didn't respond, which wasn't surprising. I could tell from where I was standing that he was dead.

Rossiter knew it, too. I wondered how long he'd known. And I wondered if he might be the one who'd killed Briney while "questioning" him.

If that was what had happened, Rossiter was a good actor. He'd given no indication that anything could possibly have been wrong. He'd seemed sure that everything was just fine.

But I'd seen enough killers to know that a lot of the time they were indeed expert actors, most of them better than the people who traveled around presenting "Selections from Shakespeare," or "Scenes from *Uncle Tom's Cabin.*" The deaths of others didn't affect them in the least, so they had no feelings to hide.

"You don't have to shake him again, Rossiter," I said, but by then Rossiter was already on his way out of the cell.

"I'll have to arrest the fella who beat him," Rossiter said.

He slammed the cell door shut and locked it. I don't know why. Briney wasn't going anywhere.

"You can't arrest one of my men," John said, and I have to admit I liked him for speaking up. "We do not know that he is responsible for what happened to that man in there."

"Mallory knows who beat the hell out of him. And I'd say the beating is what killed him. Damnation, man. Look at his face. That beating probably damaged his brain some way or other."

I still wasn't convinced that Rand was the guilty party. I couldn't help wondering if Rossiter had something to do with it.

Whatever had happened, I felt a little bit responsible. Maybe Steffens had been right about me. If I'd just gotten back to the bunkhouse a little sooner last night, Chip

Briney would have been alive now. And even if Rand hadn't killed Chip with his fists, I was still at least a little bit to blame. I'd let Briney go with Rossiter.

Briney's death in itself was bad enough. What made the situation even worse was that now Briney would never tell me or anyone who'd asked him to start the fire in the stable and to whom he'd given his "sacred word" for protection.

Rossiter looked at me, his face set in hard lines. "I hope you don't think I had anything to do with this, Mallory. It's like I said. I didn't touch the boy. And I'll have the doctor come check him out to prove it."

"No one is accusing you of anything," John told him, cutting off any answer I might have given. "If you will simply release the body to us, I'll see that Briney receives a decent burial."

It gave me a kind of funny feeling to think that Briney and Jake would be buried on the same day, maybe even side by side, in some little California town that neither one of them had ever heard of a few weeks earlier.

"I'll have to let the doctor have a look at him first," Rossiter said. "If he decides this is murder, I can't let you have the body."

"It wasn't murder," I said. "It was just an

accident."

Unless Rossiter was involved. Whatever he might have done would have been deliberate.

"An accident," Rossiter said. "Well, maybe the coroner will see it that way, and maybe he won't."

"And maybe there'll be some questions about how many bruises the kid got after you took him away from me."

Rossiter looked at me with a dark light in his eyes, and for just a second I thought he might hit me or go for his gun. Then the light faded and he shrugged.

"If there are," he said, "I'll answer them."

I needed to get back to Starcrossed. "John, you can tell me what the doctor says about Briney here."

If Rossiter had beaten Briney, it would come out sooner or later, and I'd deal with Rossiter then. I told Rossiter and John that I'd see them later, and left the jail.

As I drove the buggy back to the track, I thought over everything that had happened so far, trying to see some kind of pattern. If one existed, I couldn't spot it.

Tess O'Neill had been kidnapped in an attempt to force me to poison Starcrossed, but whoever was supposed to give me further orders, not to mention the poison, had disappeared, along with Tess.

Something had been done to Starcrossed, but nobody knew what or why. Jake Duncan might have figured it out, but now he was dead.

Chip Briney had set fire to the stables, but nobody knew why. Or rather, somebody did know, but finding out wasn't going to be easy. Maybe it was going to be impossible.

And although Jake had died in the fire, Starcrossed hadn't. From what I'd gathered, the groom who'd led Starcrossed out of the burning stable hadn't seen Jake at Starcrossed's stall, which led me to believe that Jake was already dead or unconscious and lying out of sight when the groom got there.

I believed that Mitch Clarey was mixed up in things, too, some way or the other. Jake was the one who'd called my attention to him, and Jake had been taken out of the picture.

There were a lot of different threads dangling there, but there was nothing to tie them together.

And what about Harry Wilhelm? What the hell was he doing in California? No matter how hard he tried, Harry would never convince me that he was there just for the race. During the time we'd worked together, I'd never known him to show any interest in horses or horse racing. If it had been anybody other than Harry, I might have thought he was there for some innocent purpose. But not Harry. I knew him too well. He was up to something.

Finally, and this was the thing that seemed most important of all, though nobody else appeared concerned with it: Who the hell had shot me last night at the stable?

And why?

I didn't know, but I was sure as hell going to find out.

When I got back to the track, I delivered the buggy and the instructions to Carrouthers at the pavilion and started toward the stables, still not sure what I was going to do next.

But I didn't have to make a decision at the moment. The Boss had made it for me. The next person I saw was Sam Evers, walking up to me and wearing a big grin.

"Hey, Dev," he said.

I stopped and looked him over. He was an earnest young man who wore wool suits even when the sun was delta-hot, a Southern descriptive I'd picked up during my time as a prisoner during the war. Not that

Sam, at twenty-two, knew anything about a war that was near twenty years behind us. Well, he knew what he'd heard, and in the South that would have been plenty. All one-sided, too. But he never brought it up in our conversations, and neither did I. For the most part I just wanted to forget it.

"I got here quick as I could," Sam said. "The Boss sent me as soon as he heard from you. He said you'd be needing a partner." He shrugged. "Didn't say why."

"I lost the one I came with," I said.

He shook his head. "Dang. That's bad."

Dang was the worst word I'd ever heard him say. His father was a preacher, and some of his teachings had stuck with Sam. In the bow tie he wore with his suit, he looked about fourteen years old. The middle-parted, slicked-down hair didn't give him any more authority, either.

"I didn't mean it was your fault," Sam said, turning his bowler hat in his hands. "I know as well as anybody that you take care of your partners."

"That's all right," I said. "No harm done."

I didn't mind him saying it. It *was* bad. Partners are important. Even the ones you hate, you have to get along with. You don't want somebody who might need to save your life resenting you. If that happened, they might be a little slower on the draw than they needed to be when the time came to pull your ass out of the fire. That happens in war, men not saving unpopular comrades. And it happens when you're a government agent, too. So you try to have a good relationship with your partner, and when he's in trouble, you help out the best you can. You sure don't lose him on the damned train, the way I'd lost Tess.

"You look like you put up quite a fight," Sam said. "What happened?"

"Well, let's see. First I got shot. Then I hit my head on the ground when I fell."

I didn't say that I was pushed. No need to make myself appear any more incompetent than necessary.

"The Boss didn't really give me any details about what was going on or why we're here," Sam said. "Things must be pretty rough."

That was typical of the Boss. Send a man off to do a job and not even let him know what the job was.

"Let's go have a lemonade," I said, "and I'll tell you what I know."

THIRTEEN

I'd worked with Sam Evers only once before. It had been one of his first assignments, and like a lot of youngsters he overdid everything in his attempt to be sure that he didn't make mistakes. Which naturally led him to make more mistakes than he ordinarily would have.

We'd been tracing some counterfeit bills, and after a little over a week, we'd finally gotten a tip that the men we were looking for had a little press set up on the second floor of an old house in one of the rough sections of New Orleans, of which there were many. We went there, and I led the way up the rickety stairs.

There was a noise behind a door in a little hallway, and I figured it must have been made by the men we were looking for. I told Sam to stay back and to the side. Then I kicked in the door.

Sure enough, the counterfeiters were on

the other side. One of them was working a small printing press, but the other one was ready for us. Maybe somebody had told him we might turn up. Or maybe he'd heard us coming along the hall or up those damned stairs. At any rate, for whatever reason, he had his pistol out and ready.

I saw him and hit the floor. Sam hadn't stayed back and to the side as I'd told him. He'd decided that I needed help, so he rushed into the room right behind me. Naturally, he was the one who got shot.

The counterfeiter didn't get another chance to shoot anybody, as I killed him before he could pull the trigger a second time. The other man in the room was no trouble at all. He was down on his knees with my pistol to his head. He was begging me not to kill him while the noise of my first shot was still ringing in our ears.

Sam wasn't hurt too badly, but he was sorry that I'd had to kill a man because of his overeager behavior. I was sorry too, and I hoped he'd at least learned a valuable lesson from the experience.

While we sat at the refreshment stand and sipped the cool, sweet lemonade, I told him everything I knew. I also suggested that he find himself some different clothes.

"You're going to suffocate out here in that

rig," I said. "And you'll get ribbed for looking like a dude by half the cowboys working here."

He grinned and told me that he knew he wasn't dressed appropriately.

"I didn't have time to get any new duds before I got on the train. The Boss told me to get here as quick as I could, so that's what I did."

"We'll find you something. I want you to spend the afternoon mingling with the people who've come to see the horses. You'll be looking for Mitch Clarey. You think you can recognize him?"

"Red hair, skinny, your height, shifty eyes. That's about all you told me."

"That's about all the description we've got."

"You said Clarey used to be an owner. What about some of the other owners? Wouldn't they be the ones who'd stand to profit if Starcrossed lost the race or wasn't able to run?"

It was something I should have thought of sooner. I'd been so intent on the small circle of people I was acquainted with that I hadn't branched out and investigated some of the larger group that was associated with the race.

"You're right. I'll get started on that right

now. If you come across Clarey, don't try to brace him. Just keep an eye on him and let me know who he talks to, what he does, and where he does it."

"Right. What about clothes?"

"Let's go over to the bunkhouse and see if we can find somebody your size."

We were about to leave the table when Amanda walked up.

"Dev," she said, not even looking at Sam, "they're going to bury Dad this afternoon. Will you be at the funeral?"

Her voice trembled, but she was able to get the words out, and she didn't start crying.

"I'll be there," I told her. "I'll come by for you, and we'll go together." She nodded, and I introduced her to Sam. "He'll be helping me find out who killed Jake."

At the moment, Sam didn't look like a crack investigator. He looked as if someone had hit him between the eyes with a nine-pound sledge. Mark down another conquest for Amanda, and yet another cast member for the meller-drama.

"I'm pleased to meet you," Amanda said, and Sam took her hand. I was afraid for a second that he might kiss it, but he didn't. He held it and told her the pleasure was all his, which it obviously was, and then he let

142

it go. Reluctantly, but he did release it.

After Amanda left us, I said, "You'd better close your mouth, Sam. Lots of flies around a stable, and you never know what they've stepped in."

He shut his mouth so fast that his teeth clicked together.

"I, uh, she . . ."

"Mitch Clarey," I said. "Red hair, shifty eyes. Remember him?"

"I remember. Sorry, Dev. I guess my mind wandered."

"I guess it did. Meet me back here at noon, and we'll see about those clothes then. And we'll have something to eat before the funeral."

I could tell he wanted to say more, probably ask me about Amanda, but I didn't wait to hear. I was going to talk to a few of the owners.

Steffens had gotten over his anger with me, or at least he pretended that he had. Which made it even harder for me to apologize, but I did it anyway.

"I shouldn't have said those things earlier. I was upset with myself as much as with you. And you had a point. If I'd been a little more diligent, maybe Jake would be alive."

Steffens puffed out his chest a little and

said, "I was a bit hasty, too. I know you're doing all you can."

"I'm going to do even more. I want you to introduce me to some of the owners."

"Surely you don't think they had anything to do with the fire."

It was another hot day, and a hawk was circling above us, his outline hard and clean against the bright blue of the sky. The cowboys were practicing their acts in the infield, and I could hear the catcalls when one of them dropped the pistol he'd been twirling. I don't think I ever saw anybody, much less a cowboy, twirl a pistol except for show. But it was something the public expected.

"I don't know what to think," I told Steffens. "I just know that two men are dead and that something has to be done about it."

"The owners aren't at fault. They're some of the most respected men in racing."

"And we both know how respectable the racing business is."

He gave me a sour grin. We'd already had that conversation.

"I'll introduce you," he said.

Earl Frame was known to everyone as "Big Earl," and with good reason. He was a large man — tall, wide, and thick through the middle — with black hair on his head and on the backs of his hands. If one of his horses got hurt, he could probably pick it up and carry it over the finish line.

His wife, Nola, was a tiny woman with delicate features, who was dwarfed by her husband, and the whole time I was in California, I never heard her say a word. That was because she never got much of a chance, not with Big Earl around. He talked fast, he talked loud, and he talked mostly about himself.

"Yessir, I've been raising horses for nearly twenty years, and if there's one thing I know, it's racing. That's why I tell you that beyond any question my horse is going to win that race come Saturday. If you want to get a bet down now, you'll bet better odds than on the day of the race."

His horse was Wonderment, a Thoroughbred from the same line as Starcrossed, and one Big Earl had plenty of confidence in. Wonderment was fast, I'd been told, good in the sprint and a strong finisher. But of course Big Earl would have an even better chance to win the race with Wonderment if Starcrossed wasn't running at all.

"Thoroughbreds are fine horses," Big Earl continued. He sat in an oversized chair that

I thought must have been built especially for him. "Make no mistake about it. They can run, and run fast. But not all of them have enough stamina for a long race, and we'll be running a mile and a quarter. Wonderment has more stamina than Starcrossed, and that's why he's going to win. You'll see, Mr. Mallory. You'll see."

He held a thick cigar, and smoke curled up from the end of it. The smell of it filled the covered owner's box in the grandstand where we sat. It was a pleasant smell, unlike the odor of Rossiter's cigar. But then Big Earl had probably paid a lot more for his.

"You seem mighty confident," I said.

"Confident? Oh, I am. I am. And I've put my money where my mouth is. My bet is already down."

Big Earl stared at the glowing tip of his cigar. Satisfied that it was still burning properly, he stuck it in his mouth and took a couple of satisfied puffs, blowing out more white smoke that drifted away and above his head.

Steffens had told me a little about Big Earl's financial condition. It was a lot shakier than he'd like for anyone to think. If you looked past the big cigar and all the talk, you could see that the knees of his suit were shiny, that his shirt cuffs were a little

146

bit frayed, and that his shoe leather was worn. If he'd bet a bundle on the race, he could be ruined if Starcrossed won.

"And you're not worried that something might happen to your horse?" I asked.

"Hell, no." He looked at his wife. "Excuse the language, Nola, dear." She smiled at him, and he went on. "Why should I be worried? If there's a horse that gets hurt, it'll be Starcrossed. That's what that fire was all about, wasn't it? And isn't it your job to prevent that sort of thing?"

I said that it was. "But I can't be everywhere."

"Nobody can, and nobody blames you, I'm sure."

Carter Steffens does, I thought, and maybe I blamed myself a little, too. Big Earl's insinuation was that he did, as well, but that he might have been happier if the outcome had been fatal for Starcrossed. At this point, I was feeling too bad about things even to take offense.

"Did you know a cowboy named Chip Briney?" I asked.

"The one who started the fire? If I didn't know better, Mallory, I'd say you thought I had something to do with that. I knew this little visit wasn't some kind of social call."

I didn't bother to lie to him. I said, "It

wasn't. What about Briney? Did you know him?"

"Never heard of him before. I don't mingle with the cowboys. They're here to put on a show, and that's fine with me if it brings more bettors to the race. But I don't have any interest in meeting them."

He might even have been telling the truth. With men like him, seemingly so talkative and open, it was hard to know for sure. They could lie as easily as most men told the truth.

"How about Mitchell Clarey?"

"I've heard of him, naturally. He's not the kind of person that I'd ever spend any time with."

Again, he seemed truthful, but it was hard to tell for sure. I thanked him and Nola for their time. Nola smiled and nodded but said nothing. Big Earl wished me good luck.

"And put your money on Wonderment," he said. "You can't go wrong that way. You can trust me on that."

I told him I'd consider it, but I'd never put money on a horse race. I couldn't afford it, and I knew too much about how crooked things were.

And I didn't trust Big Earl one bit.

Mrs. Ellie Vernon was five years widowed

and ten years past her prime. That didn't keep her from being coquettish. She batted her faded blue eyes, twirled her blue parasol, and smiled hopefully at me, as if she thought I might be a qualified suitor instead of a man interested in finding out if she'd had a hand in murder.

"I declare," she said, sounding like someone just off the old plantation, "I don't know why someone like you would be interested in a lady like me."

"I'm always interested in beauty," I said, "wherever I find it."

Never let it be said that I didn't know how to use flattery when I thought it might help, at least with women. I'd always found it next to impossible to flatter men like Carter Steffens or Big Earl.

"Oh, you," she said. "You're just leading me on. I know what you're up to. You're trying to get me to talk about Belle."

Belle was her horse, another Thoroughbred, and one that some people thought was faster than Wonderment. Results seemed to prove that they were right. The two horses had met in four races, and Belle had won three of them, contributing to Big Earl's current financial troubles.

"More than that," Mrs. Vernon continued, "I think you'd like to find out if I started that fire just so Belle could win all that wonderful money."

"Did you?" I said, thinking that Mrs. Vernon could never have done anything like that herself, but that she was just the kind of woman who'd be able to twist Chip Briney around her little finger and get him to offer his "sacred promise" not to tell about anything she asked him to do.

Mrs. Vernon simpered. "Now surely you don't mean that you really think I'd start a fire in the stables, Mr. Mallory. You know I'd never do such a thing. I wish you hadn't asked. It was quite ungentlemanly, and it makes me think less of you."

"Then you'd probably think even less of me if I asked you if you knew Chip Briney."

"Why not at all. I did know him, the poor sweet thing. I hope he's being treated well in the local jail. I have a weakness for cowboys, Mr. Mallory, especially young ones. They bring out my motherly side. I hope he's not really guilty of setting that fire the way they're saying."

"It doesn't much matter if he's guilty or not," I said. "He's dead."

It was cruel of me to put it so bluntly, but I wanted to see her reaction. I got more than I bargained for, as she burst into tears. She folded her parasol and hit me on the shoulder with it.

"You beast! Liar!"

I took the parasol away from her before she poked me in the eye.

"It's true," I said. "He died in the jail."

She snuffled three or four times, then reached into a small reticule that dangled from her wrist. She brought out a delicate, lacy handkerchief and dabbed at her eyes. When she was satisfied that they were dry, she put the handkerchief back into the reticule and reached for her parasol. I handed it over, and she clutched it to her.

"Chip was a dear, sweet young man. I liked him, but I would never ask him to do anything so underhanded as to burn that stable, not to win a stupid old race. I want you to find out who killed him."

"I plan to," I said, but I was afraid that I already knew.

FOURTEEN

I didn't bother to talk to any of the other owners. Steffens had told me that nobody else's horse stood a chance against Starcrossed and that if Starcrossed were eliminated, Wonderment and Belle would easily beat any of the others in the race.

Of the two owners I'd seen, Big Earl Frame struck me as the kind of man who'd do whatever it took to win, and Mrs. Vernon was far too familiar with Chip Briney for my liking. Either she or Big Earl might have bribed Chip to start the fire in the hopes Starcrossed would be killed or injured, but I was pretty sure they'd never have deliberately killed Jake Duncan. Or Mrs. Vernon wouldn't have. Big Earl was another story.

"Mr. Mallory?"

The voice came from off to my left, and I turned to see who was calling my name. It was Natalie Davis, the reporter that all the cowboys found so attractive. And I couldn't blame them. She had the kind of face that a lot of men dreamed about, innocent and knowing at the same time, with a pair of blue eyes that you could get lost in if you weren't careful, not that you'd mind if you did. She wore low-heeled boots, a brown riding skirt, and a blue man's shirt. It looked a lot better on her than it would have on any man I ever met.

"Mr. Mallory, I wonder if I could talk to you for a few moments."

There wasn't a man around who wouldn't give her all the time she wanted. That was probably a big advantage in her profession.

"What would you like to talk about?" I asked.

"About the fire, and about Chip Briney. Privately, if possible."

I looked around. People milled about, taking in the sights and trying to get a glimpse of some of the horses. It was too late for that this morning, but nobody seemed discouraged. I didn't see anything of Sam Evers.

"We could go to my tent," I said. "If you wouldn't feel uncomfortable."

She smiled. It was a nice smile. "I don't let things like that bother me, Mr. Mallory. In my job, I've had to be alone with strange men in a number of different places."

"So you think I'm strange?"

"Of course I do. You're a government agent. I've never talked to one of those before."

"You're about to," I said, and I led her to the tent.

It still smelled musty, and the single cot looked a little unkempt. While I'd taken the trouble to make it up that morning, I'd lost interest in doing it in the military fashion. There was no other place to sit, so we sat next to each other on the edge of it. She had a notebook and a pencil to write with.

"To begin with," she said, all business, "I'd like to know what you think about the death of Mr. Briney."

I asked what she meant by that.

"It's my understanding that he was badly beaten. Do you know if that's true?"

I wondered who she'd talked to, not that it mattered much. I said, "It was an accident."

"That he died or that he was hurt so badly?"

It wouldn't do anyone any good for me to start parceling out the blame. I couldn't be sure that Rand was guilty of anything, not with Rossiter in the picture, but I wasn't going to blame Rossiter, either, unless I could come up with some kind of tangible evidence against him.

"Just an accident," I said.

Natalie put the pad in her lap. "You're not being much help. I can't write a story without some more details."

"I can't help you with the story." I tried to sound as if I cared. "Briney admitted that he started the fire, and he was taken to the jail. He was dead when I went there to see him this morning. That's about all I know."

"And of course you have no idea why he might have started the fire."

"I have some ideas, but that's all they are. They aren't for publication in your newspaper. You've been talking to a lot of people, and you might know more than I do. Maybe you even know something that would help me."

She gave me a speculative look, as if she wasn't quite sure she could trust me. That was all right. I wasn't sure she could trust me, either.

"What do you know about Marshal Rossiter?" she asked after a couple of seconds.

"Not very much. He seems to know what he's doing."

"Do you think he had anything to do with Briney's death?"

"I think he's a violent man who's trying

to rein in his impulses."

"That's not much of an answer."

"I don't seem to be helping you with your story, do I?"

"Certainly not as much as I'd hoped. What do you know about a man named Mitchell Clarey?"

I tried not to look surprised at the mention of his name. "Clarey? I might have heard something about him."

Natalie laughed. "You're a caution, Mr. Mallory. You know very well who I'm talking about. How could you not, considering his reputation?"

"I know the reputation, but I've never met the man."

"You should. He's quite interesting. He's someone who stands to profit quite a bit from the demise of Starcrossed, and he's been involved with at least one racetrack fire in the past."

That was a piece of information that hadn't been in the Boss's book. I asked about it.

"It was a few years ago. He'd lost all his own horses, thanks to reckless betting and overconfidence. He was almost penniless, and to collect the insurance on his stables, he burned them to the ground. It might have worked, but someone saw him leaving and turned in the alarm in time to save the stables."

If Clarey had been tried and convicted of something like that, there would have been a record of it, and the Boss would have known.

"Not that I doubt the truth of the story," I said, "but has Clarey ever been to prison?"

She shook her head. "No."

"But you said there was a witness who saw him start the fire."

"That's right. However, the witness didn't testify against him."

"Why not?" I asked, though I thought I might have a pretty good idea.

"Because the witness disappeared. Most people assume he was murdered, but no one could prove it."

"And Clarey got off scot-free."

"You're right again, Mr. Mallory. No wonder you're a government investigator."

"You're making fun of me now, Miss Davis."

"I would never do that, Mr. Mallory. And please call me Natalie. I believe we know one another well enough by now. After all, we've been sitting in this tent together without a chaperone for several minutes now."

"Fine, Natalie, and you can call me Dev."

We were getting downright friendly. "Why did you bring up Clarey in the first place?"

"Because I think he's up to something. He wouldn't be here otherwise, and I know he's bet a considerable sum of money on the race."

I looked at the ground and thought about Tess. The thought that Clarey might have her twisted my gut. No matter how much I tried to tell myself that Tess could take care of herself and that she'd been aware of the risks we were taking, I couldn't quite get over the feeling that I was somehow to blame for her situation. I wondered if Sam had managed to locate Clarey.

Natalie touched my arm, and I looked back up and into her blue eyes.

"You went away somewhere," she said. "I was getting a little worried."

"I'm fine. I was just thinking about Clarey."

"And did you come to any conclusions?"

"I believe you're right," I said. "He's up to something."

"Do you know what it might be?"

"I'm not sure." That was close enough to the truth to pass for the real thing. "But whatever he's up to, it's not something likely to be of much help to Starcrossed."

Natalie was silent for a moment. Then she

said, "I think you know more than you're telling."

I didn't deny it. I just sat there.

She smiled. It was a knowing smile, not an innocent one.

"I didn't really expect to find out much from you," she said. "You have a job to do, and it doesn't involve telling a reporter anything you know. But I would appreciate it if you'd tell me the story, or as much of it as you can, when all this is over."

That wasn't asking too much, and I was glad to agree. I just hoped that things turned out well enough to make the story worth telling.

"I'll even buy you a good meal," I said.

"I'm taking that as a promise."

I would have been willing to promise her a few more things, but I didn't get the chance. Just then Boots Donovan stuck his head into the tent.

"Mallory! I've been looking all over the damn place for you." He noticed Natalie. "Begging your pardon, ma'am, but we got us a problem."

"What?" I said.

"Some young fella lyin' under the grandstand with his head bashed in."

My stomach felt hollow. "What's he look like?"

"Dressed up like some Eastern dude."

I stood up, bent a little under the low canvas of the tent.

"Excuse me, Natalie. I have to go."

I didn't listen for her reply. I brushed past Boots and headed for the grandstand to see about Sam Evers.

FIFTEEN

It was Sam's bowler hat that had saved him.
It was caved in on one side, and it had
absorbed some of the force of the blow that
had struck him. Even at that, he wasn't feeling exactly frisky.

He was laid out in the shade of the grandstand, not moving at all, when I got there.

"Who found him?" I asked Boots.

"One of the cowboys, Gidge Taylor, came
back here to have a smoke in the shade. Saw
him lying there stretched out and thought
he might be taking a nap. But then he
noticed that there blood."

Boots pointed to Sam's white shirt collar.
There was blood on the hat, too, but it was
too dark to show up much.

The grandstand above us was quiet. Most
of the crowd who'd come out in the morning to see the horses work out had left and
gone home. They'd be back tomorrow, hoping for a glimpse of Starcrossed or one of

the others. They'd been so busy concentrating on the horses that they'd missed the little drama taking place beneath them.

I knelt down by Sam and felt for a pulse in his neck. It was there, slow and steady, and I felt myself relax a little. I asked him how he was feeling. His eyelids flickered, but they didn't open.

"Brains is addled," Boots said. "I've seen fellas get like that when they've been kicked in the head by a cow or a balky mule. Brains don't hardly work right for a while."

He didn't add that sometimes nothing worked right ever again, and not just the brain. I guess he figured that he didn't have to tell me that.

"Any idea what happened?" I said, standing up.

"Not a bit of one. Gidge found him like that, and that's all I know. All Gidge knows, too. We thought we'd better let you know instead of that Rossiter fella. Don't any of us think much of him, not after what happened to Chip."

"You think that was Rossiter's fault?"

"Don't know. Could be. Could be Rand's fault. But I don't like that Rossiter anyhow."

"You did the right thing. I know this man. Can you help me get him to my tent?"

"Don't know that we oughta move him.

Sometimes that can be bad."

I knew he meant well, but I wanted Sam out of sight, and I wanted to get some medical attention for him. Private medical attention. Steffens had a doctor ready to go whenever he needed one.

"Get a wagon," I said. "We'll take the chance of moving him."

"Looks like he oughta have some say in what we do."

"He's not able to say a damned thing. Now go get me that wagon."

Boots gave me a hard look, but I gave him one right back. He dropped his gaze.

"And send somebody for Steffens's doctor," I said. "Have him come to my tent."

Boots looked up. He wanted to argue some more, but he must have seen something in my eyes that changed his mind. He went off to find a wagon.

I knelt down beside Sam again and asked him if he could hear me. This time he got his eyes open, but he didn't say anything.

"This is Dev," I told him, in case he couldn't see me. "You've been hit on the head, but you'll be fine." Even if it wasn't true, it was the right thing to say. "I'm going to put you in a wagon in a minute and take you to my tent. You just rest here until we get ready to go."

It wasn't as if he had much choice other than resting. He certainly wasn't going anywhere, not if he had to do the walking.

I stood up and rolled a cigarette. My hand was steady, which surprised me a little, considering how upset I'd been just a little while ago. I'd been afraid that Sam would be dead. I'd already lost one partner. It just wouldn't do to lose another one.

I heard a step behind me and turned fast. My .44 was in my hand by the time I was facing Natalie Davis.

"Is he all right?" she asked, looking down at Sam. She was as cool as if I'd been holding a carrot instead of a lethal weapon.

"He'll pull through." I holstered the .44 and took a drag on the cigarette that I still held between the fingers of my left hand.

"Who is he?"

"A friend of mine."

She looked at me with those dangerous eyes of hers.

"Mind if I have a smoke?" she asked.

I handed her the makings. "Help yourself."

She tapped the tobacco into the paper expertly and pulled the bag shut with the drawstring between her teeth. She tossed the bag to me. I caught it and put it in my pocket, and by the time that was done, she'd wet the paper with the tip of her tongue, rolled the cigarette, and twisted the ends. She was very good.

I struck a match with my thumbnail and waited a second for the sulfur to burn off. Then I held the fire to the cigarette and lit it.

She inhaled like she knew what she was doing and blew the smoke out in a long white streak.

"You didn't mention that you had any friends," she said, putting an emphasis on the last word. "What kind of friend is he?"

"He works with me."

"Not very good at it, is he?"

I shrugged. "He's young. He's still learning."

"He's not going to get much older if he's not more careful."

She dropped the cigarette to the ground and crushed it out with the toe of her boot. I flicked my own smoke to the ground and stepped on it as well.

"I don't suppose you want to tell me what happened," Natalie said.

"I'd like to know that, myself. Sam's not in any condition to tell me right now."

"So you have no idea what happened to him."

"Somebody hit him."

"You know that's not what I meant."

I knew, all right, but I wasn't going to say any more. I'd already told her the truth, and if she didn't want to accept that, too bad.

"You're upset because I followed you," she said.

She was right about that, but I shouldn't have been surprised that she'd trailed along. She was a reporter, and she knew there must be a story of some kind, thanks to what Boots had said.

"You don't have to worry," she went on. "I won't be putting anything about this in the paper. For that matter, there won't be anything about your other friend, the one who died in the fire."

That surprised me. "Why not?"

"Because Steffens controls the editor, and the editor controls the news. Oh, there'll be something about the stable fire, and maybe even something about the cowboy who started it, but it will be played down. Steffens doesn't want people to think they might get hurt if they're around the track, and he certainly doesn't want anything printed if it might keep people away from his big race."

She sounded resentful, which was only natural if she was interested in doing her job and doing it right.

"If the editor won't print the story, why did you bother to talk to me?"

"I was hoping that I could get something into the paper later, after the race. There's something bad going on out here, and I know it. If it's as serious as I think it is, it's the kind of thing that will get reprinted all over the country. If that happens, it might get noticed by someone important, and it might get me a job on a bigger newspaper." She grimaced. "It's not easy for a woman to get on with one of the better papers. I'm looking for some help."

The wagon rattled up. Boots was driving it. He got down and walked over to where Natalie and I stood. He stopped when he got near, took off his hat, and held it in both hands. Being around a woman as good-looking as she was puts a man at his best or worst. Beauty isn't always easy to deal with.

I knew he was hoping for an introduction, so I said, "Miss Davis, this is Boots Donovan, one of the best wranglers ever to straddle a horse. Boots, this is Miss Davis, a reporter for the Corvair newspaper.

"I'm mighty pleased to meet you, ma'am," Boots said.

"And I'm pleased to meet you," she answered. "I'm sorry I can't stay around for conversation, but I have to get back to the newspaper office and write an article for tomorrow's edition."

"Not about this," Boots said, looking at Sam.

"You don't have to worry, Mr. Donovan. It won't be about this."

She left, and we both watched her walk away.

"Mighty pretty woman," Boots said.

"Yeah. Now help me get Sam in the wagon, and be careful with him."

"If he don't come out of it, it'll be because we moved him."

"It's my responsibility," I said. "Now give me a hand."

He didn't want to, but he did.

Back at the tent, we carried Sam inside and put him on my cot. The doctor was waiting for us and started his examination as soon as we had Sam situated. I sent Boots for another cot. When Sam recovered he'd be staying with me. I'd lost my privacy, but I didn't have much choice in the matter. I wasn't complaining. I'd needed some help, and the Boss had sent someone. It was just too bad that Sam was already out of commission.

"How about it, Doc?" I said when he'd

finished examining Sam, lifting his eyelids, talking to him, and trying to get him to talk back.

The doctor was a little man, not much over five feet tall, and not much bigger around than a pine sapling, but he looked tough as a whip. He had sad eyes, and I knew he'd seen a lot of sickness and death at one time or another over the course of his career.

He closed his medical bag and said, "He's concussed. He got hit pretty hard, and he doesn't need to be moving around."

"We had to bring him here. We couldn't just leave him lying where he fell."

"I understand that. But that's enough of that sort of thing. Don't move him again. He needs to stay right where he is for a while."

"Is he in any danger?"

"Not unless somebody hits him again." He gave me a look as if I were personally responsible for what had happened to Sam. In a way, I suppose I was. "He'll be all right after a couple of days."

"When can he talk?"

"Oh, he can talk right now. Probably doesn't feel like it, though. You might want to let him rest."

"Can I leave him alone here in the tent? I

don't know that I can find anybody to nurse him, and I have to go out this afternoon."

"I think he'll be all right as long as he doesn't try to get up and walk around. You'll have to bring his meals. He won't need much for a while."

I said I'd take care of the meals, and the doctor left. I went over to the cot. Sam was lying there with his eyes closed. His breathing was regular and slow. For all I knew he was asleep, but since the doctor had said he could talk, I thought I'd give it a try.

"How are you, Sam?" I said.

"My head hurts like hell," he answered. His words were a little slurred, but I could understand him with no trouble. I knew he must be hurting, or he'd never have said "hell." "Somebody hit me on the head."

I was glad he knew what had happened. It meant that his mind was clear.

"Damn," I said. "I'd never have figured that out."

"Not funny, Dev."

"Sorry. Do you feel well enough to tell me about it?"

"No. I feel like six pounds of shit in a five-pound bag." He moved a little on the cot. "But I'll try anyway."

I'd never heard him say "shit" before. He was still a little addled, no question.

170

And he hadn't opened his eyes. I knew he didn't feel like going on, but I didn't try to stop him. I wanted to know what he had to say.

It wasn't too long in telling. He'd talked to someone who'd seen Mitch Clarey hanging around one of the stables. He'd gone to look for Clarey and spotted him headed toward the grandstand.

"I followed him, but I must not have done a very good job of it. He spotted me."

Clarey hadn't appeared to be upset that Sam was following him, however. He'd stopped and confronted Sam, then asked what he wanted.

"I told him I needed to talk to him, and he suggested that we meet under the grandstand, where it was less public. He went on ahead of me. I thought he might run off, but he didn't. He was waiting for me when I got there."

I thought I knew the rest of the story. He'd let his guard down, and Clarey had clobbered him. But I was wrong.

"It wasn't Clarey who hit me. We were talking, and someone came up from behind me. Quietly. I didn't hear him. The next thing I knew, it was like my brain exploded, and then you were telling me I'd been hit on the head. Heck, I knew that."

Heck. Sam was feeling better.

"What were you talking about?"

"I told him he looked familiar and that maybe I knew him from somewhere. He thought that was funny because he said he'd never seen me before in his life. I told him that I'd seen him with a woman, and he didn't like that much. He asked me to describe her, but I didn't get a chance. That's when I got hit on the head. You ever been hit like that, Dev?"

"Sure, kid. And shot a few times, too. You'll get over it."

"Is that a promise?"

"That's what the doctor said. You just have to take it easy for a few days."

"I won't be much help to you, will I?"

"Don't worry about it. You've already helped."

"I don't think so. Clarey knows we're onto him, and that's no help at all."

"He doesn't know who you are. That'll worry him, maybe enough to cause him to make a mistake. That's when we'll get him."

"You don't really believe that, do you?"

"Sure I do," I lied.

SIXTEEN

We buried Jake Duncan on the side of a hill just outside of town. A few cottony clouds floated in the blue sky, and occasionally one of them would shade the ground and move over the mourners, putting them in shadow. I could smell the ocean, but I couldn't see it. I would have had to climb to the top of the hill for that, but I wasn't interested. I could also smell the fresh earth from the newly dug graves, a smell I was all too familiar with. And would get even more familiar with when it came my turn to be planted.

Just about everybody associated with Star-crossed had come to see Jake buried.

Prince John was dressed all in black, as were Liz Hawes and her mother, though neither of them looked the least bit sorrow-ful. They appeared undisturbed by anything resembling emotion, actual or feigned, and the black clothing only emphasized their cold beauty.

Carter Steffens was rigged out in the proper garb as well, befitting his role as chief stockholder and general manager of the track, though he looked uncomfortable in it. He was an old athlete, and he hadn't yet gotten old. Funerals probably reminded him that he wouldn't always be as vigorous as he now was, and he wouldn't like that thought at all.

Others, like Donald Sterling, Starcrossed's official trainer, wore their everyday outfits. I didn't make much of that, since hardly anybody had brought mourning clothes along. They were going to a race, and they'd never expected to be attending a funeral. Somehow, however, Prince John's cousin Richard Caldwell had found the appropriate clothing. He stood as close to Amanda as he could, though she didn't seem to know that he was anywhere around.

The grooms were there, in their working outfits, and I saw Chance Oliver, the jockey who would be riding Starcrossed in the race. According to Jake, he and Oliver had become good friends, though I hadn't seen Oliver around the track very often.

A group of cowboys stood off to one side with Boots Donovan, still looking like he was in charge. Even Rand, the cowboy responsible for beating up Chip Briney, was there, and I thought it might be a good idea to talk to him later.

Marshal Rossiter was there, too. I thought that was because we'd be burying Chip Briney as soon as Jake was in the ground. Rossiter always dressed in black, I supposed, so he was always ready for a funeral.

The preacher, who'd never seen Jake in his life, talked a little about what a fine man Jake had been. It was all true, but the minister didn't know it. When he was finished with that, he read a few verses from the Bible about the sun going down and rising again, and then the ones about the valley of the shadow of death and fearing no evil.

I wondered if Jake had feared evil when he went into the stable last night. Maybe that was why he had gone, because of some fear or suspicion. But just what evil had he feared? That was something I'd have to find out.

While I was wondering about that, hardly listening to the preacher's voice, Harry Wilhelm, the man with the distinction of having worked for the Boss without giving up his criminal career, walked up the hill and stopped beside me. He didn't say anything. He just nodded to acknowledge my presence and kept a solemn look on his face.

I didn't believe he was feeling solemn any more than a Texas jackrabbit would have, but one reason he'd been good in the spying business was that he could make his face into just about any kind of mask he chose. The only time I'd seen genuine emotion in it was when his brother was killed.

The preacher finished whatever he'd been saying, and a couple of men lowered the wooden box that held Jake's remains into the grave.

Amanda stepped to the graveside and tossed a rose on top of the coffin as it went down. I didn't know where she'd gotten the flower. She held herself rigid and her face was pale and blank. Caldwell touched her elbow, but she shook him off.

When the coffin was in the ground, the men who'd lowered it began to shovel dirt into the grave. I could hear the clods hitting the top of the box. People started to crowd around Amanda to offer their condolences, and I turned to Harry.

"What are you doing here?" I said.

"Can't I grieve for a dead man?" Harry said, all the solemnity gone from his face as if it had never been there. He was the old charming Harry again, but he wasn't fooling me in the least. I could see right through the charm and into the rotten heart of him.

"You didn't know Jake," I said.

"Now why would you say that, Dev? You don't have any idea who I know. Now if you'll excuse me, I'll offer a few poor words of comfort to his daughter."

He walked away as coolly as a deacon who'd just filled an inside straight. I was a little disgusted to see that Amanda managed a weak smile for him as he approached, and that it changed to a more genuine smile when he talked to her. I wondered what the hell he hoped to get from her. Harry didn't speak to people he didn't want something from.

But if the sight of him and Amanda bothered me, it bothered Richard Caldwell even more. He kept trying to nudge himself into the conversation, but Harry kept maneuvering his body between them so that Richard never got a chance to say a word to Amanda.

It would have been funny if it hadn't been so pathetic. Richard looked as if he might burst into tears at any second, and I wouldn't have been surprised if he had. He was so ineffectual that Amanda seemed to have forgotten that he was even there.

Other people stopped to offer Amanda their sympathies, and she acknowledged all of them with a nod or a word, but Harry never left her side. Each time that Richard made a move to get his own words in, Harry blocked him.

I knew Harry was doing it deliberately, but I wasn't sure why. Maybe he simply didn't like Richard. Or maybe he saw Richard as some kind of serious rival for Amanda's attention. Harry knew people and he should have known he didn't have to worry about Richard ever getting anywhere with Amanda. The only serious rival to Harry would be the prince, who was talking to Liz Hawes at the moment. Liz seemed to enjoy the attention, and her mother was almost smiling. But not quite. I'm not sure it was physically possible for her to smile. I'd certainly never seen her do it.

Because Harry was irritating me almost as much as he was bothering Richard, I decided to walk over to the grave and do something about it.

Harry, looking over Amanda's shoulder, saw me coming toward him. Just at that moment, Richard tugged at his sleeve.

Harry, whether because he was upset to see me or because he was tired of toying with Richard, gave Richard a quick, hard elbow to his flabby midsection.

Some bulky men are graceful. They're good dancers and light on their feet. Richard wasn't one of those men. He stumbled backward, tripped over his own feet, and started to fall into the open grave.

But he hadn't let go of Harry's sleeve. He had a good grip on it, and he was hanging on tight to prevent himself from going over the edge. Harry was at least as big as Richard, and more solid, so he would have been a pretty good anchor if someone hadn't given him a little shove.

I didn't see who did it. There were several people near Harry, and it could have been any one of them. I was sure it was accidental, just something that happened in the confusion that Harry himself had created.

So Harry stumbled into Richard, and they both went over the side of the grave and fell in.

I could hear them scuffling around, but I couldn't see because the mourners, no longer mourning, gathered around and blocked my view.

I shouldered my way through the crowd and had a look. Both men were on their feet. Harry was hitting Richard steadily, alternating his punches, one to the face, the next to the belly. Richard's hapless attempts to block the blows were almost comical. His nose was bleeding, and he had a cut under one eye. He was going to be a mess, even if someone stopped the fight immediately.

But nobody was inclined to do that except Amanda, who was yelling at both men to stop, without any effect. Some of the cowboys were already starting to pull out their money and place bets on the outcome.

So I figured it was up to me to do something. I jumped down into the grave, landing on top of the casket between Harry and Richard. My feet slipped in the loose dirt that had been thrown on top of the casket, and I was unsteady for a second. Harry took advantage of that and hit me on the right cheek.

The punch stung me and knocked me aside. My shoulder throbbed when it hit the dirt, and I thought it was time to end things before they got even uglier. I slid my hand into my pocket for the knucks, but Harry knew that trick. He grabbed my wrist and trapped me with my hand inside my pants. With his free hand he aimed another blow at my head.

He didn't deliver it because Richard stuck his arm in the way to protect me. Or maybe he was trying to hit Harry. If so, he wasn't successful at it, but he did give me time to put a knee into Harry's balls.

I wasn't gentle about it. Harry released

my wrist and crumpled to his knees. He held himself up with his arms and started gagging.

"Get out of here," I told Richard.

A couple of men heard me, and they reached down to give Richard a hand, which was a good thing. I was sure Richard couldn't have climbed out on his own. He had enough trouble clambering up the side of the grave as it was.

I knelt down beside Harry, who had stopped gagging. He was just breathing hard now.

"How're you feeling, Harry?" I said.

He managed to get his head up far enough to look at me.

"You're a real bastard, Dev."

"You shouldn't pick on the young ones, Harry, especially somebody like Richard. You could have killed him."

"Serve the little turd right if I did."

I took his elbow and helped him to his feet.

Hands reached down, and we climbed out of the grave. It had been an undignified exhibition, but nobody seemed to mind. If nothing else, we'd given them a bit of excitement and relieved any gloom that they might have felt.

I looked around for Amanda, wanting to

apologize for my part in this mess, but she was talking to Richard, who looked as happy as I'd ever seen him, so I didn't bother them. I wanted to talk to Harry, anyway.

Now that the excitement was over, some of the people were leaving. They didn't intend to stay for Chip Briney's burial, which would follow shortly.

I got Harry off to one side. He was brushing dirt off his clothes with his hands, all the while muttering uncomplimentary things about my character and upbringing.

"Harry," I said, "what the hell are you really doing here in California?"

He stopped brushing at his clothes and dry-washed his hands to get the dirt off.

"You still work for the Boss, am I right?"

I nodded. It wouldn't do any good to deny it.

"I thought so. Maybe that's why you're so suspicious of me. Working for that man makes you suspicious of everybody. But I'm just here to see the race, Dev, nothing more than that. Why else would I be here?"

"That's what I'd like to know. Where were you when the fire started last night?"

He gave me one of his smirks. "That's the kind of question a gentleman doesn't answer."

"You never could give a straight answer,"

I told him. "You've always got to be a prick, even when you don't need to be."

He smirked again. "If I didn't know better, Dev, I'd think you were accusing me of something. I'll forgive you, though, since I know you lost a friend in that fire. But I didn't start it. I didn't have a thing to do with it, and you have my word on that."

Harry's word. I tried not to smirk myself as I thought about how much that particular commodity was worth. I didn't want to get into another fight. My shoulder was already bothering me, and I didn't want to cause the wound to start bleeding, if I hadn't already done that. So I just said, "I'll trust you on that, then, Harry."

"Of course you will. You know me, Dev, as honest as the day is long."

I didn't grin this time, either. I laughed out loud, which was hardly appropriate for the circumstances. We were at a funeral, after all. Harry looked hurt.

"We've known each other for a long time, Dev. I don't know why you don't trust me."

"Gee, Harry, I can't imagine." I walked away, toward another part of the small cemetery, to the spot where they'd be burying Chip Briney.

SEVENTEEN

The cowboys all stayed for Chip's funeral, and so did Amanda. Richard stayed, too, but I thought that was only because Amanda was there. Everyone else left except Rossiter, who stood near a stunted oak tree away from the grave.

The preacher didn't have much to say about Chip, but nobody seemed to mind. He finished with his few words about him and started to read the Scriptures.

"Just a youngster," I said, glancing toward the grave.

The breeze rustled the leaves in the oak, and Rossiter looked at me with narrowed eyes.

"If you think I killed that kid, you have it all wrong, Mallory. He died in my jail, but that's all. I still think your cowboy did it."

I'd been thinking about that, myself. Rand had beaten Briney pretty badly, but I didn't believe he'd hurt him enough to kill him.

I'd seen men beaten much worse than Chip get up and have a drink before riding home on horseback. They'd wake up the next morning to do a full day's work.

Of course I'd also known a single blow, landed in just the right (or wrong) spot, to kill a man. I'd have to put some more thought into Briney's death.

"Seems like everybody's accusing me of something this morning," I said. "It must be the way I look."

The marshal nodded. "I saw you and that fancy fella talking a while ago, after you stopped his fight. What's he got to do with all this?"

"Harry? Nothing," I said, though I was far from sure of that.

"Well, somebody had something to do with it." Rossiter looked at the small group gathered around the preacher. "I'd have thought more of them would stay for the burying."

I didn't ask why he thought that. "He was just a cowboy, not part of the money crowd. And he burned down the stable."

Rossiter shrugged. "I guess that would make a difference. People don't have a lot of forgiveness in them."

"Even if they forgave him, he was a hired hand who worked for the prince. That's all he meant to them."

"If you say so. I think I'll go pay my respects."

Rossiter walked past me and went over to stand beside the preacher, who was still reading from his black Bible. Rossiter took off his black hat and held it with both hands on the brim.

The preacher finished his reading, and the group broke up. Richard stayed with Amanda, and I started after the cowboys and Rand.

I seemed to be making friends wherever I went this morning. Maybe I could do the same with Rand, who was walking a little behind everyone else, except for Boots, who was beside him. The two of them were talking, their heads close together as if they didn't want anyone to overhear them.

I walked over and joined them, taking one last look back. The grave diggers were filling the hole where Chip Briney was taking his last rest. They'd finished with Jake's while Chip was buried, and a mound of raw earth lay atop it. Rossiter watched them work, a lonely figure in black. No one was near him, and I was the only one who'd spoken to him that day.

Richard Caldwell helped Amanda into a carriage that I was certain he'd rented for the occasion, probably just so that he could ask Amanda to ride with him and get her to himself. Maybe he was smarter than I'd thought.

Rand and Boots didn't look any happier to see me than Harry and Rossiter had been. Rand looked downright frightened, as if he thought I might take the knucks to him again.

I put on a friendly smile. It didn't help. Rand sped up, trying to avoid speaking to me.

I let him go and said to Boots, "Is something wrong with him?"

"You might say that. He's heard you think he's the reason Chip died. He thinks you'll get him tossed in jail."

I looked down the hill. Rand had caught up with the cowboys, some of whom had already swung into the saddle. None of them spoke to Rand. He got on his own horse and rode away.

Boots shook his head. "He don't put much faith in the law. He's scared of going to jail."

"So Rand doesn't want to meet up with a bully like himself?"

Boots thought it over. "You could put it that way. Anyway, he's probably feeling guilty. If he didn't kill Chip with that beating, who did? Rossiter? What are the chances of a marshal going to jail?"

"It's happened."

"Not very damn often. And half the fellas Rand works with think Rand did it, maybe more of 'em.

"So they're shutting him out."

"Yep. Not a one of 'em said a word to him today."

"You don't seem to be shunning him."

"Hell, I don't think he killed Chip. And if he did, it was just because he was mad as hell about Jake and that fire. I was pretty mad, myself. I don't blame Rand for what he did. Jake was a friend of mine."

We'd reached the bottom of the hill, where our horses were tied to the fence. We had to be careful where we stepped because most of the horses that had been there had left behind tangible evidence of their presence. It was also sniffable evidence, and flies buzzed around the odorous, still-fresh piles.

The fence went only a few yards on either side of the little gate. The fence was incomplete, and I thought it might never be finished. It wasn't keeping anybody in, and those on the outside didn't particularly want to get in unless there was a funeral.

"Jake was a friend of Chip's, too," I said.

"I know that. Sure seems funny to me that

Chip would've started that fire."

I told him that it sure seemed funny to me as well. But that was just one of several things I couldn't figure out. I grabbed the saddle horn and pulled myself up on the little cayuse.

"If you hear anything," I told Boots, "anything that would help me with why Chip started the fire, I mean, you'll let me know, won't you?"

"Sure will. But I doubt anybody'll be doing any talking about it."

"There's another thing," I said.

"What's that?"

"I'd like to know who the hell shot me."

"Can't blame you for that," Boots said.

Sam Evers was sitting up on the side of the cot when I got back to the tent. He looked a little ragged. His neatly parted, slicked-down hair was sticking out all over the place, and he was trying to smooth it down with his hands when I got inside. It wasn't helping much.

"Hey, Dev," he said, sounding sheepish. "I must have slept the whole time you were gone."

"No harm in that. It's probably the best thing for you."

"I do feel a whole lot better. I seem to

remember saying some things I shouldn't have said."

"I don't think you confessed to any serious sins."

He grinned. "That's not what I mean. I . . . might have used some bad words."

"They're just words, Sam. And I don't remember any of them anyway."

"I sure hope not. I don't know what would make me say things like that."

I would have told him that it was natural under the circumstances, but it probably wouldn't have helped.

"I haven't been much help to you, either," he said. "All I've managed to do so far is get my head stove in."

"Not your fault. I should have warned you about Mitch Clarey."

"Why? Didn't the Boss tell me when I signed on that everybody I'd meet on the job would be dangerous? Even the people I was supposed to trust?"

The Boss told everybody that, and there was plenty of truth in it. I was ashamed of myself for not having thought of it in a different connection. I trusted Tess O'Neill as much as I trusted anybody I knew. But what if she'd gone over to the other side? What if she'd gotten off that train willingly because she was part of the plot to stop Starcrossed from winning? I didn't think that was the case, but there was a lot of money involved in the outcome of the race, enough money to tempt anybody, maybe even Tess.

"Do you know Tess O'Neill?" I asked Sam.

He shook his head, then regretted having done so. He put his hands to his head to steady it. After a second or two he said, "I've heard of her, but I've never met her. She's Secret Service."

"Sometimes we cooperate with the Service, and they do the same with us. Tess was my partner on this job before you got here. She's the one I lost."

"Oh. I'm sorry. I guess you haven't found her yet."

"No, but I will."

I hoped I sounded as if I believed it. So much had been happening that I hadn't really had a chance to do much about finding her. Telling myself that she could take care of herself wasn't a lot of help.

Sam looked down at the cot where he was sitting. There was a piece of paper there that I hadn't noticed before. Sam picked it up and looked at it.

"Somebody must have brought this in while I was asleep," he said. "And I didn't even hear him. Do you know anybody named Franklin Givens?"

I put out my hand. "Let me have a look at that."

He gave me the paper. I didn't know the handwriting. It said: "Crown Hotel. Room 200. Tonight at 8:00. Franklin Givens."

It was the same name I'd been given before, but a different hotel. I had no idea what was going on. The only thing I knew for sure was that I'd be at the hotel that night at eight, ready for anything.

EIGHTEEN

A little after dark I was in the bad part of town. Not the shabby part where the Hotel Royale had been located, but the part that was a step down from that. I'd spent a lot of time in the bad parts of towns here and there, and I was accustomed to the down-turned eyes and the furtive looks, to men sleeping in alleys, to the soiled doves who had descended to the last rung of the ladder before taking whatever final step there was for them. So I wasn't bothered by the smell of garbage or the occasional drunk weaving down the middle of the street with a bottle of cheap whiskey clutched in his hand.

I found the Crown Hotel at the end of the street. It sat a little apart from the other buildings, and it looked as if it had been there longer than any of them. A good strong wind might push it over.

When I went inside, the desk clerk hardly

bothered to look up from his yellowback he was reading by the light of a lantern hanging from the wall behind him. He was old, with thin white hair on his head. The hair growing out of his ears was somewhat thicker. He had sleeve garters on a shirt that had once been white but was now a dingy gray. I stood in front of the desk and waited for him to acknowledge me. When he didn't, I said, "I admire your choice of reading material, but don't you think it would be a good idea to ask if I'm looking for a room?"

He stuck a creased and dirty envelope in the book to mark his place, then closed the book and laid it carefully on the counter.

"You like yellowbacks?" he said.

I nodded. "I sure do."

"You look sort of like a yellowback hero yourself."

He was fishing for something.

"Fella like you," he said, "wouldn't be looking for a room in a place like this. You look too prosperous. So you must be looking for somebody."

"Not bad. If those yellowback heroes ever need an assistant, you'd fill the bill. I'm looking for Room 200. Franklin Givens."

"Him and that woman? They don't look too well-fixed, and she was a little flummoxed when they signed in. You want to see 'em?"

"If they're here."

"Hell, I don't know if they're here. You think I keep up with the comings and goings in this place? I sign 'em in and take their money. After that, I don't give a damn. You can go knock on the door if you want to. Or just barge on in if it ain't locked. Just don't cause no trouble. I don't want to be bothered. Just want to read my book in peace."

Nobody in this part of town would want to be bothered. People would want to get along quietly and not call attention to themselves, especially not the kind of attention that somebody representing the law was likely to pay.

I thanked the desk clerk, but he ignored me and picked up his book again. I went up a short, rickety stairway to the second floor. The door to Room 200 was on my left at the top of the stairs. The 2 was hanging upside down, held only by one nail.

The hallway smelled musty, dusty, and unclean. There was no light, but a thin yellow band showed around the edges of the door to Room 200. I knocked.

Footsteps crossed the floor, and the door opened. I'd expected to see Mitch Clarey, but I was looking at someone else, someone

I'd seen once before. He didn't look nearly as dapper as he had the first time, at the stable where I'd bought the cayuse. His suit was soiled, and he'd lost the cravat. Lost the spats, too. Red scratches traveled down his left cheek, and his right eye was swollen and half-closed. He was holding a .44 in his right hand, and it was pointed at my belt buckle.

I could have had a gun in my hand, too, but I didn't want to risk shooting Tess if she was in the room. So I just looked at the man and waited.

"Come on in, Mallory," he said, motioning with the pistol.

He stepped to the side, and I went past him into the room. On the washstand there was a lamp, and Tess was lying on the bed. Her eyes were closed, and her head lolled to one side. She was wearing the same dress she'd had on when we'd been on the train, but it was as much the worse for wear as the clothing worn by the formerly dapper gent behind me, the one who was still holding his pistol in a steady hand. Her wrists were crossed and bound, and so were her ankles.

"You can take your pistol out of the holster and lay it on the floor," the man said. "Slow. And don't use more than two fingers."

I did what he said.

"Now move away from it."

I did that, too, and he came over and kicked the pistol under the bed where Tess lay.

"If she's hurt, or dead, I'll kill you," I said.

"Mighty tough talk for a man who's not even holding a gun. Anyway, she's not dead. She's not even hurt. She's just asleep."

I went over to the bed without asking permission and checked Tess's pulse. It was strong and steady. I lifted one of her eyelids. The pupil was dilated, and she didn't move. I turned to the man with the gun.

"You gave her a shanghai."

"Damned right, I did." He touched his free hand to his face. "You see these scratches? She got away from us once. It's not going to happen again."

I smiled. Tess wasn't as easy a mark as they'd thought she'd be. I thought back to what the desk clerk at the Hotel Royale had told me. He hadn't said that Clarey had left the hotel with his "wife." Tess must have gotten away from them somehow, but they'd caught up with her.

"You said *us.* Where's your partner?"

"That's none of your business. All you have to do is listen and do what I tell you."

There wasn't much chance that the last part of his order would be carried out, but I thought it might be a good idea to listen. There was a wobbly straight-backed chair near the washstand, so I sat down in it, crossed my arms, and said, "I'm listening."

"Good. You already know what you have to do to get the woman back, so I won't go into that."

"You might as well. Maybe I've forgotten."

"You're going to poison Starcrossed. It's simple. You can go wherever you want to in the stables, so it won't pose a problem for you."

"You've already tried to poison him once."

"I don't know what you're talking about, Mallory."

"And you tried to kill him by burning the stable."

"Have you lost your mind? We didn't have anything to do with that."

He could have been lying, but I believed him. After all, if he planned to make money on the race, he wouldn't want Starcrossed dead in a fire. He'd want him to run. I'd have to find out how that fit with the idea of my poisoning Starcrossed, however.

And if Givens was telling the truth, it would explain some things. It would mean that there was more than one group working against Starcrossed, and that while they had the same purpose, neither was acquainted with the other. I wondered if they'd thought of getting together. It might make my job easier if they would. On the other hand, it might not.

"You don't happen to know who was responsible for the fire, do you?" I said.

"No, and I don't care. What we're here to settle is how and when you're going to do your part."

"What makes you so sure that I am?"

He gestured toward Tess with the pistol, then brought it right back to bear on me.

"She's what makes me so sure. I had you come here to meet me so you could see that we have her and that she's healthy. But she won't stay that way if you give us any trouble."

He thought he had me. Maybe he did. I said, "Where's the poison?"

He reached inside his suit coat with his left hand. The pistol in his right didn't waver. He brought out a small glass vial.

"It's right here," he said. "All you have to do is pour this in Starcrossed's drinking water. We'll let you know when. That will be the end of it."

"No, it won't." I nodded toward the bed.

Tess lay still as death, the lamplight playing on her face. "What about her?"

"Once Starcrossed has been taken care of, we'll tell you where to find her."

"And you expect me to believe that?"

"Why wouldn't we do what we say? We'll have what we want, and we won't be needing her."

Which was precisely why they might kill her. Why bother leaving her alive to testify against them in case they were ever caught? They'd have to stay around to collect the money they'd bet on the winner, and she could identify them.

For that matter, why leave me alive? I had a feeling I might get a bullet between my shoulder blades as soon as Starcrossed was dead. That made me think of something else that had been bothering me.

"Won't Starcrossed be scratched from the race? How do you expect to collect if he's dead?"

"He won't be dead. Just sick. The doctors will think he has some kind of lung trouble." He shook the vial. "And this stuff won't leave any traces behind."

"He'll still be scratched."

"No. If you give this when we tell you, Starcrossed won't be affected until after the race starts. He'll even cross the finish line.

He just won't be first."

I'd heard a few stories about such potions in the few days I'd been around the track, but most people didn't believe they existed. However, nobody had been able to figure out what had caused the ruckus with Starcrossed yesterday. Maybe it was something similar to the liquid in the vial that I was looking at now.

Or maybe an infected fly had bitten the horse. I wasn't an expert, and I couldn't say. What I did say was, "I'll take your word for it. What we have to do now is work out some kind of satisfactory way for this to go forward."

"We've done that. I've told you the plan."

"But I don't like it. I have to get some kind of guarantee that my partner will be returned safely. I'll tell you what. I'll just take her with me now."

He smiled. "And what would guarantee me you'd carry out your part of the deal?"

"The same thing that would guarantee you'd carry out yours."

"What would that be?"

"Mutual trust."

His face split into a wide grin.

"What's so funny? You expect me to trust you to return my partner, but you don't want to trust me to do my job. I don't see the difference."

"Maybe you don't. But you're not the one holding the pistol. That's all the difference you need to know about."

He was right about the pistol, but I didn't agree with the rest of it. I didn't think he'd care whether I agreed or not. He wasn't going to change his mind, and I hadn't expected him to. I was just trying to give myself time to think of what I was going to do. Unfortunately, I hadn't come up with any good ideas.

There was a chest of drawers against the wall behind him. He moved to it and said, "I think our talk is over with. I'm going to put the poison down here on top of this chest of drawers, and then I'll move over by the window. You can pick up the vial on your way out."

I had to do something soon or it would be too late. Since I didn't have a plan, I'd have to do something reckless and stupid and risk getting Tess killed, the very thing I'd wanted to prevent by putting myself in this situation to begin with.

I snatched the lamp from the washstand and threw it at him.

I was hoping he'd be so surprised that he wouldn't be able to get off a decent shot. He was surprised, all right, but he pulled the trigger anyway.

The bullet buzzed by my ear as I threw myself sideways from the chair.

The lamp missed him and hit the wall, breaking into fragments and sending coal oil splattering on the wall, floor, window curtains, and Givens's clothing.

And then things started to burn.

Givens snapped off another shot in my direction, and I hoped he wouldn't think to shoot Tess before I could do something about him.

His clothing caught fire about that time and distracted him, though maybe not as much as the chair I threw at him. I hit him dead center, and he fell backward, crashing into the window and falling through it to the outside.

It wasn't much of a fall, and I didn't know if he'd be injured, but I didn't care. I had other things to worry about. Such as the fire.

I took Tess off the bed and laid her on the floor. Then I jerked the filthy coverlet off the bed and started beating out the flames. It took me a few minutes, but there hadn't been much oil in the lamp, and I managed to get the fire out before it caused any serious damage.

The window curtains were ruined, and the

walls and floor were scorched, but hardly anybody who stayed in the Crown Hotel would care about little things like that. The smell of burning cloth and wood filled the room, but that was actually an improvement. I thought I should charge the hotel's owner a fee.

I tossed the coverlet back on the bed and retrieved my pistol. Then I went to the window and had a look outside. I was careful to stand to the side and peer around the edge rather than to stick my head out in case Givens was standing below, ready to blow my head off.

But he was gone. A couple of people passed by, unconcerned. If anyone had heard the gunshot or seen Givens fall, there was no evidence of it. In this part of town, random gunshots wouldn't be uncommon, and nobody would be surprised if someone fell from a window.

I holstered the .44 and checked on Tess. She was still unconscious, so I untied her hands and feet, and hoisted her over my shoulder. She was light as down as I carried her out of the room.

Nineteen

The desk clerk looked up from his yellowback when I got to the lobby.

"You was a little noisy up there," he said. He caught sight of my female burden. "And what in hell are you doing with that woman?"

"I thought you didn't pay any attention to the comings and goings around here."

He opened his mouth, then closed it and chewed on his lower lip while he thought things over.

"I see what you mean," he said after he'd considered it. "None of my damn business, is what you're telling me. You're sure as hell right about it, too."

I was glad that he agreed with me. "That a good yellowback?"

"Damn good."

I went on outside. The night air didn't smell any sweeter, but I was feeling much better about things now that I had Tess back. All I had to do was figure out how to get back to my horse while carrying her slung across my shoulder like a sack of cottonseed meal.

I didn't attract a lot of attention as I walked down the street. You might think that Tess and I would make an odd sight, and we did, but we weren't the first odd sight most of the people around the hotel had seen. We'd attract a few stares when we got back to the respectable side of town, I suspected, but here we were just another couple out for an evening stroll. I got a couple of glances, but nobody met my eyes, and I just kept walking.

I was so pleased with myself that I let my guard down. The Boss has talked to me about that a time or two in the past. Well, not that, exactly, but about what he calls my tendency to get cocky.

"If there's one thing wrong with the way you operate," he told me once, "it's that you think you've won the game before it's over. You need to be more careful and keep on playing until the last out is recorded."

And as much as I hate to admit it, he's right. I'll win a little skirmish and start thinking the war's ended. What I tend to do is think of the kind of people I deal with as being like rabbits or possums, running off when they're scared or turning up their toes and lying still and quiet in the hope that if they don't move, I'll go away.

I forget that I'm usually dealing with people who are a lot more like snakes than possums. And snakes are different. You can break their backs, and you can shoot off their tails, but they'll keep right on thrashing around. You can even cut off their heads, and if you're not careful, they can still sink their fangs into you and kill you after they're already dead themselves.

All of that is a long way of saying that I shouldn't have forgotten about Givens. I should have left Tess in the hotel room, where she'd have been safe enough, and gone after Givens to be sure he wasn't hanging around somewhere waiting to ambush me.

Which is exactly what he was doing, the son of a bitch.

When I walked by the mouth of an alley, I heard something move in the dark. It might have been nothing more than a dog rooting through some garbage, but it wasn't. Luckily, I wasn't so full of myself that the instincts that had kept me alive for so many years weren't completely dulled. I realized at some level that the sound wasn't made by a dog.

I didn't hesitate. I dumped Tess off my shoulder and whirled, drawing my .44 as I did.

Givens was in the alley, and he shot first. He missed.

I saw the flame from the barrel of his pistol and aimed where I thought the middle of his chest would be. I was a better shot than Givens. I didn't miss.

Givens didn't make a sound, but I heard him fall back against something in the alley, a barrel or a box, and then hit the ground.

Not having a light, I was doubly careful when I went into the alley to check on him, but I needn't have worried. He lay on his back, and he wasn't moving. Keeping in mind how careless I'd been already, I checked to be sure that he was dead.

He was. I thought for maybe a second about notifying Rossiter, but I didn't feel like explaining everything to him, and I didn't think anybody would miss Givens, at least not anybody who'd consider going to the law about his death. The desk clerk knew I'd been to Givens's room, but he would care the least of all, since I was sure he'd collected his rent in advance.

Once again the gunshots had drawn no attention. The alley was quiet, and so was the street. I looked back in that direction to be sure that nobody was coming after me. Nobody was.

I bent down and searched Givens's jacket. He hadn't had time to put the vial on the dresser, and I found it in an inside pocket. I thought it might be a good idea to take it with me. No need leaving it to tempt Mitch Clarey, should he decide to claim the body. If he had the poison, he might try to find somebody else to slip it into Starcrossed's water. For that matter he might even try to take Tess again, or someone else, Sam Evers, maybe, and make another attempt to force me to do his dirty work for him.

I put the vial into my own pocket and rifled Givens's clothing to see if there were any clues to tell me where Clarey might be hiding out. I found nothing.

It was time to leave the alley. I was glad Tess was unconscious. If she'd been awake and aware, she'd have given me unshirted hell for dumping her in the dirt of the street and letting her lie there. I'd have to make sure she never found out about it. If she had any bruises, I'd blame them on Givens and Clarey.

If I got the chance, that is. Once again, I'd gotten cocky. Sometimes I wonder if I'll ever learn. Probably not. When I got back to the street, Tess was gone.

I heard hoofbeats and turned back toward the hotel. A horseman was moving quickly in that direction, and I thought I could see someone thrown across the front of the saddle.

I'd left the cayuse a few blocks away, in a slightly better part of Corvair, because I'd wanted to be sure he'd be there when I got back. I took off at a run, and got back to him in under a minute. As soon as I was in the saddle, I tore off after Mitch Clarey, for I was sure he was the one who had Tess.

Dirt flew from under the cayuse's hoofs as I urged him forward. People got out of the way quickly when they saw me coming, though I almost trampled one drunken man who couldn't move fast enough. As it was, he got a solid bump from the cayuse's side as we rushed past him, and he tumbled ass over elbows. I looked back, and he was getting to his feet, so I figured he was all right.

The Crown Hotel was at the lower end of Corvair, and when you reached it, you couldn't go much farther and remain in the town limits. I passed a ramshackle saloon where someone was playing an out-of-tune piano and a few shacks that might or might not have been occupied. After that the street became a road that led into the open country.

The black sky was free of clouds, and the big white moon was near full. I could see Clarey ahead of me about a quarter of a mile. If I'd been on Starcrossed, I'd have caught up to him in seconds, but even the cayuse was making up the distance pretty well. He was carrying only me, and even though Tess was small, Clarey's mount was still carrying double. I knew I could catch up with him.

So did he. He turned off the trail and into a grove of trees. I went right in after him. He couldn't have been going far, not riding fast among trees in the nighttime. That was a good way to break your horse's neck, and yours.

I'd gone only a little way into the trees when I found his horse standing free. I looked for Clarey and Tess, and a bullet took my hat off before I could get out of the saddle.

I fell off to one side, hoping to make him think I'd been hit. I didn't have to fake a yell, since the fall did my wounded shoulder no good at all. What with jumping out of the chair at the hotel and now off my horse, it was taking quite a beating.

I rolled over to a tree and got behind the trunk just as a bullet thunked into the side of it and tore out a hunk of bark and wood.

The trunk vibrated, and it was about then that I realized how thin it was and how little protection it gave me.

"Mallory," Clarey said. "Is that you, Mallory?"

He knew well enough who it was. He'd been avoiding me long enough. And I supposed he didn't think he'd hit me, either.

"I have the woman, Mallory. You have to listen to reason and do what we're asking you."

He'd taken the opportunity to get Tess back, and he was going to use her against me.

If he could. I'd lost her twice now, and I was angry with myself for being so stupid. Since I couldn't beat myself up, much less shoot myself, Clarey would be a more than satisfactory substitute.

"Do you hear me, Mallory?" Clarey called. "If you don't step out from behind that tree with both hands showing and no pistol in either one, I'll put a bullet in this woman's head."

He might do it, or he might not. I tried to talk him out of it.

"She won't be any good to you if she's dead."

"To you, either."

He had me there, or he thought he did.

"Kill her, then," I said. "I don't give a damn."

I did, of course. For one thing, Tess was my partner, and a man's supposed to take care of his partner. And when you got right down to it, I was at least partly responsible for the position she was in.

But Clarey didn't know that. If he'd heard about me at all, he'd probably heard I was a cold-blooded son of a bitch who'd give up my own mother if I had to. Or I would have if she'd still been around. She wasn't. She'd died of consumption the year before the war, so long ago that even my memories of her were faded now.

"You don't mean that," Clarey said.

"Try me and see."

"I will, by God."

It was quiet in the trees, so quiet that I heard the hammer of Clarey's pistol click as he pulled it back.

It sounded loud in the silence, but not nearly as loud as the scream he emitted next.

I wasn't sure what was going on, but I knew the scream wasn't just a ploy to distract me. I was out from behind the tree and on my way to Clarey's hiding place when he screamed again.

When I got to him, Tess O'Neill had his

balls in one hand and his pistol in the other. She slammed the pistol into the side of his head, and he collapsed. She had the kindness to let go of him as he fell.

"I take it that the drug has worn off," I said, putting my own pistol back into the holster.

Tess glared at me. I wondered if she was going to shoot me.

"You bastard. You'd have let him kill me just to save that damned horse."

"That damned horse is my job. You know that."

"I also know you're not as hard as you'd like me to think. Take this pistol."

She held it out to me, and I took it as she sagged forward. I caught her in the crook of my arm and steadied her.

"I don't know what they gave me," she said, "but it was potent stuff."

"It's a good thing you recovered when you did."

"That's another thing. When I started to come around, I was lying in the street. How did that happen?"

There are times to tell the truth and there are times to lie. This was one of the latter.

"Givens carried you there when he was trying to get away from me. I caught up with him, and he threw you down."

"And then?"

"I caught up with him, and he ran into an alley."

"Did he get away?"

"No. He tried, but he didn't get far. I shot him."

Tess straightened up and moved away from me. She said, "I can stand alone now, I think. Did you kill him?"

"Yes. I checked to make sure. He's dead, all right."

"Good. He deserved it."

Her voice was hard as nails.

"What did he do to you?" I said.

"I'll tell you later. We should take this bastard to jail."

She gave Clarey a nudge with her toe. It wasn't a gentle nudge. He groaned and turned on his side.

"I'd like to talk to him before we take him anywhere," I said.

"Then tie him up. He's not as bad as his friend, but I don't like him one bit. I don't want him to be comfortable or think he has a chance to get away from us."

I got a rope from my saddle and propped Clarey against a tree. Tess held him up while I tied him to the trunk. Tess kept telling me to pull the rope tighter, and I did what she said. When I had things done to her satisfaction, Clarey still hadn't come to. His head sagged forward on his chest.

I thought it would be a while before he was able to talk, so I asked Tess to tell me what had happened to her.

"You know they gave you a shanghai on the train?" she said.

"Yes, and I figured you might have had a little nip from my flask, yourself."

"I couldn't resist. It was only a small one, but it was enough to muddle my head. Clarey and Givens were able to get me off the train, and they kept me drugged when they took me to Corvair."

I remembered Givens's face and said, "The drugs wore off, though."

"Clarey didn't think keeping me drugged was a good idea."

I grinned. "He didn't know you very well."

"No. After they untied me, I got away from them and got out of the hotel. I didn't get far, though, because I was still a bit under the weather. They caught up with me and kept me out of town for a while."

"That must be when you scratched Givens."

"No. I'd already done that. The son of a bitch tried to molest me, and I gave him something to remember me by. After that they decided to keep me in a fog. Givens

216

liked that idea. As I was going under, he put his hands on me and told me what he was going to do to me as soon as I blacked out."

Goddamn him. I hadn't been sorry that I'd killed him. Now I found myself glad I'd done it.

"I don't think he violated me, if that's worrying you," Tess said. "Clarey would have stopped him. But he handled me. I hated that."

A dark cloud passed over the moon about then, and I couldn't see what her face looked like. I thought I had a good idea, however.

"He won't be doing it again," I said.

"No. I'm not sorry he's dead, the bastard."

I told her I wasn't sorry, either. "Did you overhear them say anything that would tie them to anyone at the track?"

"No. They never talked about their scheme in front of me except to say that they needed you to 'take care of Starcrossed' for them. Have you had trouble?"

The moon came out from behind the cloud and the tree branches shadowed her face. I thought I heard Clarey moan. I looked at him, but he wasn't moving, so I gave Tess a quick summary of what had happened at the stables.

"I'm sorry about Jake. I didn't know him, but you said he was your friend. What about his daughter?"

"Her name's Amanda," I said, and I filled her in on everything I hadn't already covered.

By the time I'd finished, Clarey was awake and listening to us. He was pretending that he was still out cold, but I knew better.

"Clarey can tell us the rest," I said. "Isn't that right, Mitch?"

He must have known that his pretense wouldn't do him any good, so he gave it up. He said, "I don't know what you're talking about."

"I think you do. And if you don't tell me what I want to know, I'm going to let Miss O'Neill have her way with you. She's not real happy with the way she was treated."

"I didn't hurt her. And I kept Givens off her."

"She knows that, but Givens took too many liberties. Givens isn't here. That leaves you."

"Where's Givens?"

"You don't have to worry about him. He's not around anymore."

"I saw what happened in that alley. You killed him."

"Sad, but true. And all the while you were

stealing Miss O'Neill away from me again instead of coming to his rescue."

"I wasn't sure what was going on. I would have helped if I could have."

"I don't doubt it," I said, though I knew he was lying. He wouldn't help anybody but himself unless he saw some profit in it. "But now that Givens is gone, you'll have to tell us what we want to know."

"And if you don't," Tess said, "you'll be sorry. Not for long, though. Give me that pistol, Dev."

I handed her Clarey's pistol. She took it with a two-handed grip and pointed it at Clarey's crotch.

"If I were you, Clarey," I told him, "I'd talk. She doesn't like you, and she's still mad about what Givens did to her. I've seen her deal with men like you before. They were never the same afterward, if you know what I mean."

I hadn't actually seen Tess emasculate anybody, but Clarey didn't know that, and Tess looked very determined.

Clarey strained against the rope. It didn't give, and he sagged back against the tree trunk.

"You're both crazy."

"Maybe. But whether we are or not won't make any difference to you if she pulls that trigger."

"All right, damn you. What do you want to know?"

Tess looked at me. I said, "I want to know who else you were working with. Was it Earl Frame?"

"I wasn't working with anybody. The whole scheme was Givens's idea. He talked me into it. I didn't want to get involved, but he said we could make a lot of money if we bet on the right horse at long odds, so I went along with him. I should have known better."

It made sense for him to try to put everything off on Givens, and the story would improve every time he told it. By the time I turned him over to Rossiter, he'd probably have Givens holding him at gunpoint rather than persuading him with the talk of money.

"So you don't know Earl Frame or Ellie Vernon?"

I thought I might trick him by throwing in Ellie's name without warning, but he was too quick to fall for something as simple as that.

"I've met Frame, and I know Mrs. Vernon. She likes men, and she likes to talk. I've spent a little time with her."

I didn't ask him exactly how he'd spent the time. I wasn't sure I even wanted to

know. But now that I'd established a connection, I wanted to find out more about it.

"When's the last time you talked to her?"

"It's been a while. She didn't have anything to do with this. It was Givens, right
from the start."

"So it was Givens who hit my partner in
the head when he met you under the grandstand?"

"I didn't know he was your partner. I
thought he might be a Pinkerton. Anyway, I
didn't want him around. We didn't hurt him
much. Givens wanted to do worse, but I
stopped him. Anyway, he's the one behind
the whole thing. He ran the show."

I thought Clarey might be telling the
truth. If he and Givens had planned to make
money by betting long odds, they'd have
been betting some horse other than the
three best in the race. Maybe there was
another player in the game, someone I
hadn't even thought of.

"Which horse were you planning to bet?"
I asked.

"I don't know. Givens was going to take
care of everything. He was going to put the
money down, not me. I was just keeping an
eye on the track to make sure that things
were going smoothly. I didn't have anything
to do with the planning."

"He's not going to be any help to us, Dev," Tess said. "Let me shoot him."

Clarey crossed his legs, as if that would help.

"I don't like the idea of taking somebody's manhood away," I said.

"Fine." Tess raised the pistol so that it pointed at Clarey's forehead. "I'll just kill him, then."

"We can't just leave his body here," I said, playing along. "Somebody might find him, and he'd be one body too many, what with Givens lying back there in the alley."

"This is lonesome country. Nobody will find him, not until after the race, anyway. I think we should kill him. Even if they do find him, they won't know who shot him."

"For God's sake," Clarey said. "Stop talking like that. Don't let her kill me, Mallory. I haven't done anything to hurt her."

Aside from holding her captive for a few days, that is, and letting Givens put his hands on her. I was tempted to tell Tess to pull the trigger, and I thought she'd do it. I think Clarey believed it, too. He struggled against the ropes.

"If I knew anything, I'd tell you," he said. "It was all Givens and me. We weren't working with anybody else. As God is my witness."

Clarey didn't seem to me to have a hell of a lot of gumption. I figured that if he'd known anything, he'd have told us to save his skin. Tess seemed to have come to the same conclusion. She lowered the hammer of the pistol, and Clarey drooped back against the tree.

"We'll have to take him to jail in town," I said. "The Boss will want to press federal charges against him."

"Jesus," Clarey said. "Can't you just let me go? I'll get out of town, and you'll never hear of me again. I know what Givens did, but he's paid for that."

Letting Clarey go had a certain appeal. I wouldn't have to deal with Rossiter, and I didn't think the Boss would mind. He had plenty of other things to worry about, and as long as Tess was free, he wouldn't care about Clarey.

"What do you think?" I asked Tess. "You're the one he held prisoner."

"He didn't do anything to me. And he kept Givens from doing as much as he wanted to."

"So you're saying that we should turn him loose?"

"No."

"Why not?"

"Because I think he's a liar. You didn't

223

believe all that, did you?"

"Hell, no," I said, trying to cover my confusion. "I was just testing you. Let's get him on a horse and carry him back to town. Rossiter has a nice little jail, and only one man's died in it this week." I paused. "Unless you want to go ahead and kill him."

"No. I think he knows more than he's saying, but he's not going to tell us because he's more afraid of somebody else than he is of us. Maybe spending some time in that jail you mentioned will change his mind."

I wanted to ask her what she was talking about, but she saw the question in my eyes and shook her head.

"Later," she said. "Get him on the horse."

While Tess held the pistol on him, I untied Clarey and got him to his feet. Then I tied his hands and managed to get him slung across the cayuse. After that, I tied his feet together.

"I hope he's as uncomfortable as I was," Tess said.

"You planning to ride his horse?" I asked, wondering how she'd manage it, since she was still wearing the dress she'd had on when they took her off the train.

"I can do it."

"There's no sidesaddle."

"I can manage."

She handed me Clarey's pistol, and I stuck it in my belt. She pulled up her dress and petticoats and bunched them around her waist, holding them with one hand and arm.

"Now help me up on that horse. And stop looking at my legs."

"I apologize for that."

I helped her up on the horse, and she settled herself in the saddle, arranging the dress and petticoats as best she could.

"Make it as rough a ride as you can," Tess told me when she was comfortable. "I want Clarey to feel it."

I did the best I could.

TWENTY

Rossiter wasn't overjoyed to see me, and he was even less pleased when I told him that I was bringing him another prisoner.

"I don't want him dying on you," I said, and Rossiter gave me a black look. "He knows something he's not telling, just like Briney. We can't afford to lose him."

"It won't be my doing if he dies," Rossiter said. "And neither was the other."

He was looking at me when he said it, but I could tell his mind was elsewhere. He was dying to ask me about Tess. Well, let him die, for all I cared. I wasn't going to tell him a thing. I helped him get Clarey off my horse and into a cell.

"You can charge him with kidnapping," I said when we were back in Rossiter's office. "And interfering with a federal agent in the performance of her duties. That should be enough to hold him for a while. I might think of a few other things before the night's over."

"Federal agent? We talking about that woman outside on the horse?"

"That's right."

Rossiter waited for me to go on. When I didn't, he said, "Speaking of other things you might think of, you wouldn't know anything about the body of a fella that was found near the Crown Hotel earlier tonight, would you?"

I was surprised he'd heard about Givens already. I'd have thought it would be morning or later before he got the word.

"The Crown Hotel? Never heard of it."

"I talked to the desk clerk there. He said the dead man had a redheaded friend."

"Could be just a coincidence."

"Maybe. Not a lot of redheads around here, though."

"You'll have to talk to Clarey about it. Maybe he can identify the dead man for you."

"Oh, I've identified him. Name's Givens, Franklin Givens. Or so it says on the hotel register. And you never heard of him?"

I didn't think the desk clerk would have mentioned me. He knew how to mind his own business, or so he'd said, and I was willing to take his word for it. But when Clarey started giving out his story about

Givens having planned Tess's kidnapping, my part in things was going to come out. So I told Rossiter a cleaned-up version of what had happened.

His face got darker and redder as I went along.

"And you didn't think I needed to know any of this?" he said when I finished. His voice was tight, as if he were having trouble squeezing out the words.

"It wasn't a local matter. I handled it as I saw fit."

"Made a damn poor job of it, too. One man dead, and a hotel nearly burned down."

The fire hadn't been that bad, and he knew it. I doubted the clerk had even mentioned it to him. I didn't call him on it, however. No use in getting him any more riled than he was already.

"I have to take care of my partner now," I said. "I'll leave Clarey to you. He knows more than he's telling, and if you get anything out of him, get in touch with me."

"Yeah. I'll be sure to do that."

He wouldn't have pissed on me if I'd been on fire, but it didn't bother me. He had a right to be angry, I figured, since I'd killed someone in his town and there was nothing he could do about it.

"Thanks," I said. "I'd appreciate it."

He was too mad to answer, and I went back outside to where Tess was still waiting.

She started up with me as soon as I stepped out of the jail.

"What were you two doing in there? Having a cup of coffee and trading war stories?"

"I had to tell him what the situation was. And he already knew about Givens. I had to explain that, too. He wasn't happy about it."

"Meanwhile, I had to sit out here on this horse and have everybody that came by stare at me."

I apologized for making her wait. It would have been awkward to get her off the horse with an audience, I thought, and just as awkward to get her back on.

"I need some different clothes, I want something to eat, and I need a place to stay," she said.

"I'll take care of everything," I told her.

"You'd better," she said.

There had been races in Corvair for years, even some big ones, but there had never been a famous horse like Starcrossed in any of them, and there had never been a purse like the one involved this time. So quite naturally the town was filling up with people who were interested in the sport, those who were interested in the betting, and those who were simply curious and wanted to see Starcrossed.

"There's not going to be a vacant room in this whole town," Tess said as we rode down the street, which was still crowded even though it was late.

"There's one at the Crown Hotel," I said.

"I meant a decent room."

"I told you it was all taken care of."

Most of the people who were out walking around had never seen a woman in a dress straddling a horse, and Tess got plenty of curious stares. She did her best to ignore them, and I made sure to keep the grin off my face whenever she looked in my direction.

"And I'm not staying in any tent with you," Tess continued. "I know I'm serving my country, and I expect a little hardship now and then. But I've suffered enough on this trip. I want a room with a roof, and it had better be comfortable. And clean."

"That's already been arranged," I said. "Don't you trust me?"

She gave me a skeptical glance. "I want some clean clothes, too, and they'd better fit."

"That's been taken care of, too."

"You'd better not be lying to me, Dev."

"Have I ever lied to you?"

She didn't bother to answer that one. We'd arrived in front of the City Hotel. In spite of the fact that its name wasn't nearly as grand as those of the hotels on the other end of town, it was the best and most expensive place to stay in Corvair.

"This is the place," I said. "Now we have to figure out how to get you off that horse without giving the whole town a free show."

"You let me worry about that," Tess said, and she swung one leg over the saddle, managing to keep it under cover and hardly revealing more than an ankle.

It was a nice ankle, and she knew I'd seen it.

"I swear, Dev, a person would think you'd never been married."

I wished she hadn't mentioned that. I'd been married, all right, and it had ended badly for all concerned. It wasn't something I liked to be reminded of.

Tess slid off the horse's back without any further comment. She tied the animal to the hitch rail, looked up at me, and said, "Well? If you have everything arranged, let's go in and get me settled."

I didn't think she believed me. I said, "All right."

I dismounted, and we went inside. There was a big chandelier with lots of candles in the lobby and a clean rug on the floor. There were a couple of overstuffed chairs and a potted plant that was still green. The desk clerk had on a clean suit, and he'd even had a bath recently. Quite a change from the Crown Hotel.

I told him that Miss Tess O'Neill was registered there, and he checked his book to make sure. He probably didn't believe that there was a vacant room in the place, but I knew there was. And it wasn't exactly vacant. Tess's traveling trunk was already inside. Our baggage had been put off at Corvair when our train had gone through, even though I'd stayed aboard. I'd claimed the baggage when I got there, and I'd also rented the room and paid in advance for it to be sure it would be waiting when I found Tess.

Sure enough, to his surprise, the clerk found that Tess was registered. He gave me the room number and the key, and I led Tess to the room, which was considerably cleaner than the one at the Crown.

"This is fine," she said when we'd gone inside and she'd had a look around. "I wish I'd been here to enjoy it the whole time."

"You can get a bath here at the hotel, too,"

I told her.

She turned to face me. "Are you implying that I *need* a bath?"

"Who, me? You know that a gentleman would never imply something like that about a lady."

"You're no gentleman, Dev, and I'm no lady, but never mind that."

She went to her trunk and opened it. Maybe she wanted to make sure that nobody had stolen her clothes.

"You can go now, Dev," she said, looking into the trunk. "I'll be fine for tonight. I'll get something to eat and take that bath you suggested. Tomorrow we'll decide what we need to do next."

"Don't you want to tell me why you think Clarey was lying?"

"Tomorrow. If you haven't figured it out for yourself."

I started to say something else, but she shook her head, and I got out of there.

As glad as I was that Tess was safely away from Givens and Clarey, I knew that she wasn't really herself. Not yet. No one could recover quickly and completely from whatever kind of shanghai they'd given her, not if she'd been dosed with it several times, as Tess had been.

What bothered me was that even in her current state, Tess had figured out something that continued to elude me. I never kidded myself that I was the smartest man around, and the Boss had told me before that I was better at the physical things than the ones that involved brainpower. It was good to know that I had some usefulness.

The streets weren't quite as crowded as they'd been. I rode the cayuse back to the stables and led Clarey's horse behind. When I got back to the track, I turned the horses over to one of the grooms and checked on the security at the stable where Starcrossed was located.

According to the guard, nobody had been in or out, that is, nobody who didn't have permission to be there. I wasn't entirely confident that was true, considering what had happened the night before, so I went inside and had a look around for myself.

It was quiet except for the occasional snuffle or snort of one of the horses, and the place was filled with the distinctive smell of hay and manure. Starcrossed had a stall a bit away from the others, and he was perfectly content to be there. I was sorry I hadn't brought a carrot for him, but that might have been a bad idea. Prince John might not have approved.

It appeared that things were well in hand at the stables, so I went back to my tent to find that Sam Evers was reading one of my yellowback novels by lamplight. He'd managed to get his hair slicked down again, and he looked a lot better than he had earlier.

"Hey, Dev," he said when I came in. He held up the book and grinned sheepishly. "I hope you don't mind that I snooped around a little. I got bored, and I thought maybe you'd have something to read."

I didn't like for anyone to go through my things, but the book had been stuck right under the cot, and he must have noticed it there.

"Did you find your partner?" he said, closing the book on his finger to hold his place.

I told him that I had and gave him an abbreviated version of how I'd spent the evening.

"I wish I'd been there to help," he said when I finished. "I feel fine now. The lines in the book don't even wobble when I read them."

"Maybe you can give me some help with Clarey," I said, sitting down on my cot. "Tess thinks he's holding out on us, but she didn't say why she thought so."

"I don't see it like that," Sam said. "If

235

somebody was pointing a pistol at my head, I'd tell what I knew."

That wasn't true. If it had been, the Boss would never have hired him in the first place. The Boss was rarely wrong about the people who worked for him. Harry Wilhelm had been a mistake, or so I thought, but he was the only one I knew about.

"You're underrating yourself," I told Sam.

"Maybe. But from what I've heard about Clarey, he's not courageous. He's a race fixer, not a tough."

"If he's holding out, it's because he's more afraid of what somebody else would do to him than he is of being killed by Tess."

"What's worse than dying?"

I didn't have an answer for that one.

TWENTY-ONE

The next morning I checked the crowds around the railing for suspicious characters. I didn't see any.

Tess wasn't there. She would still be in the hotel, I thought, still recovering from her experience with Givens and Clarey. I didn't want to rush her back to work.

Amanda was there, watching Starcrossed get his morning exercise, so I went over to talk to her.

"How are you doing?" I said.

"I'll be fine, Dev. Thanks for asking. Doesn't Starcrossed look fine?"

He did, indeed. If you judged by appearances, it was hard to imagine that any horse could beat him. The sun shone on his coat, and his muscles rippled underneath the skin. He looked to be in tip-top condition for the race.

The same couldn't be said for Donald Sterling. He didn't look well at all. His face was gray and haggard, and he had trouble with his coordination. He tripped over his own feet with each step he took as he put the horse through its paces.

"What's the matter with Sterling?" I said.

Amanda didn't know. "He's been acting strangely since I got here a few minutes ago. And see how Starcrossed reacts to him? He never liked Donald as much as he liked Dad, even though Donald has been around him since he was a colt. But now he seems to have taken a positive dislike to him."

She was right. Starcrossed didn't want to be anywhere near Sterling. I hadn't noticed until she called it to my attention, but then I hadn't been standing there as long as she had. I thought the horse was upset because of Sterling's obvious physical ailment, whatever it was.

There was a murmuring in the crowd gathered along the rail, and I knew they were talking about Sterling's condition. As we watched, he stumbled and almost fell. One of the grooms went over to him, but Sterling pushed him away.

I saw John coming across the green of the infield. His face showed his concern for Sterling, and I slipped under the rail and started to where Sterling stood. He wobbled a little to his left and then fell.

The prince and I reached him at about the same time.

"What's the matter with him?" John said.

I told him I didn't know and looked around for some help. I saw Boots, who was talking to Natalie Davis, the reporter. He hadn't seen what had happened to Sterling because he'd been engrossed in his conversation. Or in his admiration of Miss Davis's charms. I waved for him to come over. He said something to her and started toward us.

John lifted up Sterling's head and called for someone to bring water. I didn't know what good water would do, but I didn't know if it would hurt, so I said nothing.

"What's the matter with Sterling?" Boots asked as he came up.

"We need to get him to a bed, and we need the doctor."

One of the cowboys brought some water in a canteen, and John put it to Sterling's mouth. Sterling managed to take a swallow, but he spit it back out.

Boots and I picked him up, with me taking the shoulders.

"My room is closest," John said, and he led the way after sending the cowboy for the doctor.

The prince had his own private quarters

in Carter Steffens's house near the track. Steffens had turned over the entire first floor of the house to the prince and moved to the second floor.

Boots and I carried Sterling into the bedroom and laid him on the bed. It was an even better room than the one Tess had at the hotel. Sunlight came in through the open window and fell in a square on the floor.

A small crowd had followed us from the track, and John went to send them away. When he returned, Amanda was with him. She wasn't looking lovestruck as she often did around him. She was too worried about Sterling and what his condition might mean. If he was incapacitated, she was next in line to become Starcrossed's trainer. It was something she wanted, but it would be quite a responsibility, even though she'd get very little credit since she'd have only one day with the horse before the race. And I knew that no matter how much she wanted to show what she was capable of doing, she didn't want anything to come to her at the expense of Sterling's well-being.

"How is he?" she said

I told her that I didn't have any idea. The doctor came in then, and shooed us out of the room.

"You need me anymore?" Boots said

I told him that I didn't and he left, no doubt a lot more concerned about finishing his conversation with Natalie Davis than about Sterling's health. None of the cowboys liked Sterling much, for which I didn't blame them. I didn't like him much, either.

Richard Caldwell was on the front lawn, smoking a cigarette. I rolled one for myself while he asked Amanda how Sterling was doing and if his illness meant that she would now be working with Starcrossed. She told him that she didn't know, and he went into a long monologue about how much she deserved the job and why she was just about the most wonderful person who'd ever walked the face of the earth.

I smoked and wondered if I'd ever been as young as those two and if I'd ever been as infatuated as Richard so clearly was.

I had been, of course, a long time ago, and it had led to nothing but trouble. Love makes fools of us all, I thought. The tobacco left a hot, bitter taste in my mouth. I threw the cigarette on the ground and mashed it flat.

On my way back to the track I met Boots and Natalie. He might have wanted to spend his time talking to her, but she had the reporter's instinct for a story. When she asked me what was going on, I told her that Sterling had taken sick and that the doctor was with him.

"What does this mean for Starcrossed?" she said.

"Nothing will change. Starcrossed will run as scheduled."

"What about a trainer? He's already lost two."

"Mighty suspicious if you ask me," Boots said. "It's like somebody don't want Starcrossed to run in that race."

Natalie gave him an admiring look, like a teacher who was willing to overlook faulty grammar because her star pupil had just solved a tricky arithmetic problem.

"You're right. I wonder why I didn't think of that."

She'd thought of it long before Boots had, I was sure. And I wondered if there was another meller-drama developing right before my eyes. She turned to me.

"That's what you're here for, isn't it?" she said. "To be sure that Starcrossed runs?"

Her tone was neutral. There was no hint of accusation in it. But I felt belittled just the same because I didn't seem to be of much help to anybody. Tess had been kidnapped, I'd killed a man, Jake had been murdered, and Chip Briney had died in jail.

Now Sterling was mysteriously ill. And I'd done nothing to prevent any of it.

"That horse is gonna run," Boots said. "Dev will see to it, won't you, Dev?"

"Damned if I know," I said, and I didn't. All I knew was that I hadn't been doing a very good job of seeing to it so far.

I was going to walk away and leave them there, but I saw Harry Wilhelm coming toward us. He looked agitated and unhappy, but when he got to where we were, he was his usual suave self, tipping his hat to Natalie and inquiring calmly after Sterling's health.

I gave him the same report I'd given Natalie, but he wasn't nearly as indirect in his response as she'd been.

"You're doing a damned poor job of protecting people around here, Dev. The Boss is going to nail your hide to the wall if you don't do better." He seemed pleased at the prospect. "I always thought you were reliable, a man to be counted on."

Everyone seemed to be concerned about how I was doing my job. I waited for Harry to go on, but he didn't say anything more. He bade us a good day and moved on to talk to Amanda. I didn't like the way she brightened when he approached, but I liked it a lot more than Richard did. His body tensed, and his damp eyes narrowed. If he'd been a snake, he'd have struck.

But as it was, he did nothing, and within a couple of seconds, Harry had Amanda's full attention. Richard was forgotten as the two of them walked away, leaving Richard standing there looking after them with such a hangdog expression that I almost felt sorry for him.

"Ain't young love wonderful," Boots said.

"Yes," Natalie said, "it is. And now I'd like for you to buy me a lemonade, Boots."

"Yes, ma'am," he said, grinning like a donkey eating an ear of corn.

They seemed to have forgotten about me. I took another look at Richard, whose hangdog look had turned to something uglier. There was nothing I could do for him, and I saw Steffens coming. I didn't want to talk to him, so I left for town. I needed to see Tess.

We sat in the hotel lobby in the overstuffed chairs and watched people come and go while I told her about the latest happenings at the track.

Tess wore a brown riding habit that nipped in at the waist. The jacket had a high collar and buttons down the front. She had on a man's bowler hat that didn't look masculine at all on her. She looked refreshed, as if the night's rest had flushed all the effects of the shanghai out of her system.

"What do you think is wrong with Sterling?" she said.

"I didn't wait for the doctor's report. I don't have any idea what happened to him. Maybe it was something he ate. When are you going to tell me why you think Mitch Clarey was lying to us?"

She looked around the lobby. Nobody was there now except us and the desk clerk. She said, "I thought you'd have figured it out by now, Dev."

"Well, I haven't. I can't see any reason to think he's working for somebody else."

"All right, then I'll give you a reason. How did he know we were on that train?"

Well, there it was. I told myself that I'd overlooked it only because it was so obvious, but that didn't make me look any smarter.

"Damn," I said. "How *did* he know?"

"Figure it out."

It didn't take much brainpower to do that. "Somebody told him."

"Now that's a brilliant answer. The question is, who told him? You said that Clarey's fixed some races, but he's never kidnapped a federal agent before. That's a big step to take. Somebody who's dabbled in small crimes isn't likely to think of something like that."

"Givens," I said. "It had to be Givens. Clarey said it was all Givens's idea. So Clarey must have been telling the truth after all."

Tess's mouth twisted. "If that's right, who told Givens we were on the train? He couldn't have known."

I couldn't come up with an answer. I said, "There are ways he could have found out."

"Really? Do you want to tell me what they are?"

It wasn't a secret that we were coming to California. Steffens knew, and so did the prince. But they wouldn't have told anyone, or I didn't think they would have. I mentioned their names anyway.

"I suppose that's possible," Tess said. "But I don't believe it, and neither do you. Besides, did they know which train we'd be on?"

The answer to that was *no.* The Boss was careful about little things like that. He'd told Steffens that we were on the way to California, but he hadn't given him a specific arrival date. He didn't like for people to know too much about the movements of his agents.

"They didn't know," I said. "So that leaves us right where we started. Givens must have found out somehow."

"From whom? Think about it, Dev. Who's the only person that could possibly have gotten hold of that kind of information?"

I thought about it, and I didn't like the answer that came to me, though it was the only possible one.

"It would have to come from somebody inside the agency."

She nodded. "That's right. Or from someone who *used* to be on the inside and still has some contacts there. Who does that leave?"

"Harry Wilhelm," I said. "Goddamn him."

TWENTY-TWO

"It doesn't have to be Harry," Tess said when she saw the look on my face, "but that's who came to mind when you told me he was here."

I'd mentioned Harry when I'd told her about the events at the track. I hadn't made a special point of his being there, just that he'd once worked for the agency and that I didn't like him. Tess had made more of those simple facts than I'd been able to do.

And what she'd come up with made sense. Harry had operated outside the law for most of his life. He was exactly the kind of man who'd plan something like the biggest race fix in history. And he was exactly the kind of man who'd keep himself in the background and get somebody else to do all the heavy lifting.

"The Boss is going to be mighty upset when he finds out," I said.

"And I don't blame him," Tess said.

"Somebody in his agency gave us up to Wilhelm."

"There are a lot of ways that could happen. Harry can be very persuasive when he wants to be."

I told her about the way he'd charmed Amanda.

"And he can be violent," I added.

I told her about what had happened in Mexico.

In this case it didn't matter whether Harry had used persuasion or the threat of violence. What mattered was who he'd used it on. I'd have to send the Boss a telegram to let him know. He'd deal with it in his own way. But I was the one who'd have to deal with Harry.

But there was something else.

"Harry's not the only problem," I said. "There are at least two groups trying to affect the race. Harry's bunch wanted me to poison Starcrossed, but the horse has to be in the race for them to collect any winnings. Givens didn't have any idea about the stable fire, and whoever set it seems to be trying to keep Starcrossed out of the race. I thought at first the two groups might be working together, but instead they don't even want the same thing."

"What's going to happen when Harry

finds out what happened to his partners?"

I recalled Harry's agitation when I'd seen him earlier that morning. I was pretty sure he hadn't heard about Givens and Clarey, but maybe he'd been worried because he hadn't gotten any word from them. They should have notified him that I had the poison and that the plan was set in motion, but he wouldn't have heard anything, since one of them was dead and the other was in jail.

"He's going to be mad. I don't know what he might do."

I thought about the time in Mexico. This time Harry wouldn't have me with him to watch him gut-shoot anybody. He'd probably want to gut-shoot me instead. Or he might gut-shoot somebody else. When Harry got mad, it was hard to predict what he might do, other than to say it wouldn't be pretty.

"I have to get back to the track," I said. "I need to get there before Harry finds out what's happened."

"Don't you think you should check on Clarey first?" Tess said. "Considering what happened to that young cowboy you told me about."

"Good idea. I'll have a little talk with him about Harry Wilhelm."

"And find out if the marshal has told anybody that Clarey's in jail. I'll go with you."

I started to tell her that she should stay at the hotel, but I knew it wouldn't do any good. Instead, I said, "I didn't bring a horse for you."

"That's all right. I've arranged for my own transportation. You can drive."

I'd seen a buggy outside the hotel. Sure enough, Tess had hired it for the day. I handed her up to the seat and got in beside her.

"Do you think the marshal has had any luck with Clarey?" Tess asked as we bounced along.

I didn't think Rossiter would even have questioned Clarey. He didn't want anybody else to die in his jail.

"Do you think he killed the cowboy?" Tess said.

I still didn't know the answer to that one. Thinking back, I didn't remember having seen any new marks on Briney. And I just didn't think that Rand had done enough damage to kill anybody. Briney's death was just another puzzle that I might never solve.

Rossiter was sitting in front of the jail, tilted back against the wall in a wooden chair. He wore the same black suit, or another one that was just the same. He didn't bother to get out of the chair when I stopped the buggy.

Then he saw Tess and leaned forward. The chair's front legs thunked on the wooden porch, and Rossiter stood up. I wasn't sure he recognized Tess. She didn't look like the same woman he'd seen last night.

"How's the prisoner?" I said.

Rossiter didn't like the question, but he answered calmly. "He's fine. I'd say he was feeling better than he did when you brought him in. He's downright chipper."

He probably thought he was safe from both Harry and from me. But he had another think coming.

I got out of the buggy and put up a hand for Tess. She stepped down lightly, and I introduced her to Rossiter.

"This is Tess O'Neill, my associate from Washington. She's working with me at the track."

Rossiter removed his black hat and looked at her carefully. "Pleased to meet you, Miss O'Neill. Were you here last night?"

"Yes, I was. But I wasn't feeling well."

"You're looking fine this morning, if you don't mind my saying so."

"I don't mind, Marshal." Tess gave me a

sidelong glance. "In fact, I'm glad someone noticed."

I'd noticed. I'd just neglected to say so, a common failing of mine.

"Have you told anybody that Clarey's your prisoner?" I asked Rossiter.

"Who would I tell? Have you told anybody? He's had no visitors."

"He's about to have one," I said. "I'd like to talk to him. There are a few things I think he'll help me with now."

Rossiter looked doubtful, but he took me back to Clarey's cell. I saw that Tess noticed his odd, crabbed walk. They went back out to the office and left me alone with Clarey. I didn't think Rossiter would mind at all spending a little time with Tess. In fact, he actually smiled once when she said something to him.

I stood in front of the iron bars of the cell. Clarey sat on his cot and glared at me.

"Have a good night?" I said.

"Good enough. The food's not bad, either. I had eggs for breakfast. Maybe I'll just stay here."

"I don't think Harry would want that," I said.

Clarey jumped as if I'd poked him with a sharp stick.

"Harry? Who's Harry?"

He tried to cover his confusion. It didn't work.

"You know who Harry is. You've been working with him to fix the race. He's the one who told you which train I'd be on and who'd be with me. The whole scheme wasn't Givens's idea. It was Harry's."

"He'll kill me," Clarey said, looking down at the floor. If he'd been feeling chipper earlier, he wasn't now. "He'll beat me to a pulp, and then he'll kill me."

"He can't get you if you're in here."

"If you think that, you don't know Harry."

"I know him, all right. I'll make sure he doesn't get to you."

Clarey looked up. His eyes were bleak. I could tell he didn't think I'd stand a chance against Harry.

"You and what army?" he said.

I touched the .44. "This one."

Clarey laughed. It was a twisted, sour laugh.

"If you believe that, you just *think* you know Harry. I saw him kill a man once for no reason at all. He'd have plenty of reason to get rid of me."

I'd seen Harry do plenty of killing, so I knew Clarey had a point. But I didn't see any reason to discourage him any further.

"Harry doesn't even know where you are,

not yet. Maybe we can keep it a secret."

"You ever try to keep a secret from Harry?"

Clarey wouldn't take comfort from anything I said, so I gave up trying. I'd learned the main thing I wanted to know from him. He'd confirmed that Harry was the problem, and now I'd have to solve it.

"How were you going to let Harry know I had the poison?"

"Givens and I were supposed to meet him this morning at the track. By now he knows something's wrong."

That confirmed what I'd already figured was the truth of the matter.

"I'll take care of it," I said.

"Yeah. Sure you will."

It was good to know that everybody had so much confidence in my abilities. Clarey had no more to say to me. He lay down on the cot and turned his face to the wall.

"I don't think Harry will be worried about Clarey," I told Tess as we drove back to the hotel to pick up my horse. "I think that he'll come after me."

"Why wouldn't he just leave town, now that he knows he's beaten?"

"Harry's never beaten," I said, remembering Mexico again. "And he doesn't like to leave the job half done. What worries me is that he might try to find some other way to make me do what he wants."

"Who else is vulnerable?"

"Amanda. He was talking to her when I left the track. They went off together."

"And that worries you?"

"Yeah," I said. "That worries me."

TWENTY-THREE

I left Tess at the hotel, but I knew she'd be out at the track almost as soon as I got back. When I arrived, I stabled the cayuse and went looking for Amanda.

I didn't find her, but I found Sam. He was out of the tent and mingling with the crowds.

"I'm fine," he told me when I asked about his head. "Never felt better."

There was a knot the size of a hen's egg on the side of his head, but it was smaller than it had been the last time I'd taken a good look at it.

"I've been looking for some of the characters in the Boss's book," he said, waving an arm to indicate the crowd. "I haven't seen any."

"They're not the ones we're worried about now," I said, and I explained the situation as I understood it.

"This Wilhelm doesn't sound like a very

pleasant fellow."

"He's as unpleasant as they come, and that's putting it mildly. He's dangerous as a rattler and twice as mean. We're going to look for him, but I want you to be careful."

"You don't have to worry about me, Dev. I've learned my lesson."

I wished I could believe him. He was just a kid. Harry would chew him up and spit him out and never think twice about doing it.

But I needed help, and Sam was what I had. Tess would be there soon, and she'd be better at the job. Harry didn't know her, and she'd be smart enough not to brace him on her own. I didn't think that was true of Sam.

"If you find Harry, you come to me," I said. "Don't let him know you're onto him. And there's one other thing. He might have Amanda with him."

Sam looked as if I'd punched him in the gut. He'd seen Amanda only once, but he'd been powerfully affected, like a lot of the men who met her. Except of course for John, the one she really wanted to affect.

"We have to stop him!" Sam said. "We can't let him hurt her!"

He was so upset that I wondered what effect Amanda might have on him if he spent some time in her company. Probably he'd be like Richard Caldwell, jealous as hell of anybody who got Amanda's attention.

"I don't think he'll hurt her," I said, trying to calm Sam down. "He might use her as a hostage if he gets desperate, but right now he's not aware of what we know."

"Not now, maybe, but what if he finds out?"

"He won't find out, not if we get to him in time." I wasn't really sure what Harry knew or didn't know, but the kid needed a little reassurance. "And you can't be the one who tips him."

"He won't find out anything from me, Dev. I promise you that. If I see him, I'll come looking for you before I do anything."

"Good. Before we start looking, let's go over to where the buggies are parked."

"Why? Shouldn't we get started at once?"

"There's somebody I want you to meet," I said.

We got to the parking area just as Tess was winding her way among the buggies and wagons and coming onto the grounds. She carried a brown parasol that matched her riding habit, and she was quite a sight. There were plenty of other women around, all of them dressed more colorfully, and Tess should have looked like a sparrow in a flock of peafowl, but she didn't. She was the one that your eyes turned to, no matter where she was.

I introduced her to Sam, who was properly impressed, but not in the same way he'd been impressed by Amanda, which was just as well. I didn't need him mooning around over two different women. One was bad enough.

After the introductions, I told Sam to cover the track area while Tess wandered around the grounds. I'd look at the stables.

"Harry might not even be here," Tess said. "Do you know where he was staying?"

I hadn't asked. I hadn't thought it was important. I'd known I needed to look into Harry's reasons for being at the race, but I hadn't had time to do any investigating. Other things had intervened.

"We'll just have to hope he's here and that he's still in the dark about what happened to Clarey and Givens. And remember, don't brace him."

"Yes, Father," Tess said.

Sam smiled.

"I'm not making a joke," I said. "I'm trying to keep you alive. You don't know Harry. I do. He's a killer."

"I'll be careful," Sam said, but Tess just

smiled.

I was happy to see that security at the stables was as good as could be expected. A guard stood at each entrance I passed, and everyone was wearing the ribbons that identified people with a reason to be there. By now I was familiar enough with the faces to be certain that so far nobody had faked a ribbon to get near Starcrossed.

Birds fluttered around the stable and congregated on the ground, where they pecked around at the droppings to see what they could find. The grounds were kept as clean as possible, but wherever there are a lot of horses, there are birds hopeful of finding something to eat. They scuttled out of my path and took off with flapping wings when I came near.

Carter Steffens was inside the stable where Starcrossed was, so I went in to talk to him and see if he knew of any developments with Sterling.

"He's sicker than a dying cat," Steffens said. I could tell that the idea of any kind of physical weakness bothered him. He still thought of himself as a vigorous athlete even if he was years past his football-playing days. "But the doctor thinks he'll pull through."

"Did he say what the problem is? Is it

something contagious?"

Steffens shook his head. "You don't have to worry about catching it. The doc thinks he was poisoned."

I touched my jacket to be sure that the vial I'd taken from Givens was still there.

"Any idea who did it?"

"Look around and take your pick. Nobody likes Sterling."

That was true enough, but why would anyone hate him enough to poison him? It seemed to me that this was another indirect attack on Starcrossed.

"Who'd profit the most if Starcrossed didn't get into the race?" I said.

Steffens didn't hesitate. "The other owners. The purse won't change even if Starcrossed is scratched. It's too late for that. You've talked to two people with the most to gain. What did you think of them?"

I gave him a summary of my impressions. When I was finished, he nodded in agreement.

"You're right about Earl Frame. He needs the money. Mrs. Vernon doesn't, but she'd like to win simply because she likes to see her horses come in first. I think she'd prefer to win honestly, though. She's not the kind to go around poisoning people or trying any other dirty tricks."

I didn't know if Steffens was being chival-rous or honest. I leaned toward honesty, as I hadn't seen any evidence that he was chivalrous.

"Do you think Earl or Mrs. Vernon could have been behind Sterling's poisoning?" he asked me.

"I don't know. How would poisoning him affect Starcrossed's chances? The race is tomorrow, so there's no more real training to be done, and Amanda Duncan can step right in and take Sterling's place for the short time that's left."

"Maybe *she* poisoned him. She'd give a lot to be Starcrossed's trainer."

He didn't know what he was talking about. Amanda wasn't that devious. She was open and direct, and she wouldn't have stooped to poison for any reason. Steffens didn't know her well, so I forgave him his ignorance.

"Besides," Steffens continued, "if she got the job, she could stay close to the prince. You must have seen how she looks at him. Maybe she thinks being Starcrossed's trainer would get her some attention. As it is, the prince doesn't even seem to know she's alive."

He wasn't as ignorant as I'd thought, and he was a lot more perceptive than I'd given him credit for.

"Speaking of Amanda," I said, "have you seen her today?"

"She was outside my house with some smooth-talking slicker when I went to see about Sterling. Why?"

"I thought she might be here with Star-crossed."

"Maybe the prince hasn't offered her the job yet."

"Maybe not," I said, thinking, *And maybe she went off with Harry.*

"You sound worried."

"I am." I told him a little about Harry. Not about Tess's kidnapping or what Harry wanted me to do, but enough to let him know that Harry might not have Star-crossed's best interests at heart. "If you see him again, let me know."

"I will. I don't want anyone like that hanging around the stables. Have you told the prince about him?"

"No," I said. "I'd better do that right now."

"He was at my house with Sterling. He might still be there."

"I'll have a look," I said.

Harry wasn't there, and neither was the prince, but the little banty rooster of a doctor was still with Sterling, who was in bad shape.

I asked the doctor how he thought the poisoning might have happened.

"Do you mean, was it an accident? Because if you think that, you're wrong. I don't know what he got in him, but it didn't get there by accident."

"Could it have been intended for one of the horses?"

The doctor looked up at me. "In the last couple of days, you've been shot, your friend has had his head bashed in, and one of your cowboys has died over at the jail. And you're asking me if this was an accident?"

What he said gave me an idea. "Do you think Chip Briney, the cowboy at the jail, could have been poisoned?"

"I never thought to check for that. That Prince John seemed awful eager for me not to say a beating had killed that kid, but he never asked me about poison. Now that you bring it up, though, I'd have to say it was a possibility. Far as I could tell, he wasn't beat up bad enough to die. But it's hard to say about something like that without more of an examination, and that prince fella didn't favor that."

I didn't ask if John had paid the doctor to rush his examination or to reach a predetermined verdict. I wondered if it was too late to check Briney for poison now that he'd been buried.

"Too late for me to do anything," the doctor said. "I'm not some big-time scientist. I'm just a backwoods doctor who's trying to make a decent living by curing folks of the croup and the epizootics."

It was already too late for Briney, too, far too late, but the idea of the poison started me off on a whole new train of thought about what had been going on.

"Let's say Briney was poisoned. He died and Sterling didn't. Why is that?"

"Because Sterling's a good bit bigger than that cowboy was. If they both got the same dose of the same thing, and I'm not saying they did, mind you, then that one in the bedroom there might survive it just because of his size."

"What did you do for him?"

"I gave him a purge. If he was poisoned, which is what it looks like to me is what happened, that's about the best I could do for him."

"Could a man and a horse be poisoned by the same thing?"

I was thinking of the vial in my pocket again.

"Sure they could," the doctor said, "but

the same poison wouldn't affect the one like the other. Why?"

I almost gave him the vial, but he'd implied that he didn't have the laboratory to analyze it, even if he had the skills, and he probably didn't have those, either.

"You don't still think this was some kind of accident, do you?" he said. "That somebody mistook a man for a horse and gave him a dose?"

I told him I didn't think that at all.

"Well, that's good. Because it didn't happen that way. It just wouldn't be possible."

I thanked the doctor for his help and left the house. I had no more ideas about where to look for Harry, since I didn't know where he'd been staying. I'd told Sam and Tess to meet me at the cowboys' mess tent to eat around noon, so I went there, hoping they'd had better luck finding Harry than I had.

But they hadn't.

Twenty-Four

Sam looked almost frantic because nobody had been able to locate Amanda, either. He couldn't even eat his beef and potatoes. He stirred them around and picked at them, but he wasn't fooling anybody.

The cowboys didn't notice Sam. Every now and then their chatter would stop, and they'd sneak a glance at Tess when they thought she wasn't looking. But Tess, unlike Sam, was always fully aware of what was going on around her. She was, that is, unless she'd sneaked a nip from somebody's drugged whiskey flask.

"What do you think's happened to Amanda?" Sam said. "Do you think Wilhelm has her?"

I was afraid that was the case, but I didn't want to let Sam know I was worried. I said, "Probably not. He'd have let us know by now if he did. He wants something from me, remember, and he'd use her against me if he could."

Sam wasn't convinced, but then neither was I. Tess said, "I think we should start asking around town. Somebody might have seen him and know where he's staying. We'll start with the hotels."

I couldn't think of anything better, so I agreed. We finished our food, or at least Tess and I did. As we left the tent, Boots Donovan met us. Natalie Davis wasn't with him, which was just as well. I didn't feel like answering any of her questions, assuming she had any.

"I been looking for you," Boots said to me. "I was asked to give you a message."

"Who's it from?" I said.

"That dude-looking fella who was talking to Amanda this morning. He said you knew him."

Harry. So he wanted to get in touch. I hoped that didn't mean what I thought it did.

"I know him. What did he want?"

"He wouldn't say. He said to tell you there was something in your tent that you ought to take a look at. It was real important, he said. A matter of life and death."

I put a hand on Sam's arm to restrain him. If I hadn't, he'd have been off at a dead run.

"Anything else?" I asked Boots.

"That was it."

"You didn't mention this to your reporter friend, did you?"

Boots reddened. "Nope. But she was with me when he said it. She left right after. Said she had to go back to town."

I hoped she'd told Boots the truth, but I didn't trust her. I'd known a reporter or two in my time, and they were always sniffing out some kind of story, even if there wasn't one. There was one here, all right, and it was the kind that could get somebody like Natalie Davis killed if she got too close to Harry.

I didn't tell Boots that. I said, "You two seem to have hit it off."

"Yeah. Well, she kinda likes the idea of being seen with a cowboy, I guess."

"And who wouldn't?" Tess said, causing Boots to redden even more.

She was trying to lull Boots, to make sure he didn't go off half-cocked like Sam was about to do.

"We need to get to the tent," Sam said, shaking off my hand. "What are we waiting for?"

"You go with Tess to her buggy," I said, "and then go back to her hotel. I'll meet the two of you there and we'll decide what to do."

Sam wasn't mollified. "What if we need to be right here?"

We'd already searched the grounds, and Harry wasn't there. It seemed obvious that he was elsewhere and that the note would tell us what he wanted us to do. I didn't want to explain all that in front of Boots, and I didn't have to, thanks to Tess.

"Dev knows what he's doing," she said. "You come with me, Sam."

Sam let himself be led away, but it was easy to see he wasn't happy about it.

"What in hell is going on here?" Boots said, looking at Sam's tense back.

"I'll tell you all about it," I said. "One of these days."

The air in the tent was hot and still, held in by the canvas. I walked over to my cot where a piece of paper lay under a small stone.

Two words were printed on the paper: TRES ROBLES.

I didn't have any idea what that meant. Harry must have thought I'd either know or be smart enough to figure it out. I was touched by his confidence in me. I picked up the paper, put it in my pocket, and went outside.

While I was standing there with the sun beating down on my head and trying to think of who to ask about Tres Robles, I saw Natalie Davis heading in my direction. I thought about ducking back into the tent, but it was too late. She'd already spotted me and started toward me. It was just as well. If anybody around the track would know what the note meant, a reporter was likely to be the one.

"I've been looking for you," she said. "I want to ask you some questions."

"About what?"

"Not what, whom."

"I've always admired people who use good grammar. About whom, then?"

"A man named Harry Wilhelm."

"Maybe we'd better go in the tent. I have something to ask you, too."

I held the flap back for her, and she went inside.

"Pick a cot."

She picked mine, which may have been a little less messed up than Sam's. I couldn't tell much difference, but maybe she could. She sat with her back straight and took her notebook and pencil out of her reticule.

"What do you know about Harry Wilhelm?" I said, sitting on Sam's cot.

"That's what I was going to ask you. He

272

seems to be quite a mystery to most people."

"You've been asking about him?"

"I was curious. Especially after what he said to Boots. I mean, Mr. Donovan."

"You can call him Boots. Everybody does."

"Then I will, too. But tell me more about Mr. Wilhelm."

"Why don't you tell me what you found out when you asked around? You might know more than I do."

She thought it over and must have decided that I wasn't going to talk until she did. She put away her pencil and notebook and said, "I told you. He's a mystery. Nobody seems to have known a thing about him until he came here."

I didn't think there was anything unusual about that, and I said so.

"You don't understand. The racing world is really a very small one. Everybody knows everybody else. Yet this Harry Wilhelm apparently shows up out of nowhere. He seems to know quite a bit about racing, but he doesn't know any of the people associated with it. He doesn't have any connections. Naturally, people are curious."

"Naturally."

"You don't have to say it that way. And I'm not talking about myself. The thing about Wilhelm is that he seems to have told different stories to different people. They don't match up."

That sounded like Harry, all right, and I thought it was a good bet that none of the stories he'd told were true. Or even half true.

"Something is going on," Natalie said, "and I don't know what it is. Too many strange things have happened, and they all lead me back to you."

I got out my makings and offered them to her. She rolled a smoke and handed them back. I rolled one of my own and lit both. We smoked in silence for a while. Then I said, "I don't know what's going on, either. I've been trying to figure it out, but I'm not having much luck."

I didn't intend to tell her about Givens and Mitch Clarey. She'd find out about them on her own soon enough. And I certainly didn't intend to tell her about the plot they were mixed up in with Harry. She might find that out from Clarey, if Rossiter let her talk with him, but not from me.

"You know more than you're telling," Natalie said.

Smoke swirled around in the tent and gathered near the ridge. I'd have to air the place out later.

"Let's just say that I met Harry a long

time ago, and that I don't trust him. We were never friends, and I don't think he's to be trusted."

"Then why would he say that he wanted to talk to you about a 'matter of life and death'?"

"That's what I'd like to find out." I took out the piece of paper and handed it to her. "Do those two words mean anything to you?"

She glanced at the paper and handed it back to me.

"Tres Robles is the name of an old ranch outside of town, from the days when the Spanish were running this part of California. There's a huge oak tree that's really three trees grown together. That's how the place got its name."

"That's all? There's nothing else out there?"

"There's a ranch house, but no one lives in it. It's been abandoned for years."

I suspected that was where Harry had been staying. It would be a good place to keep out of sight during the times when he didn't want to be seen, which would be most of the time. And the note meant that he wanted me to come there.

Natalie finished her cigarette and exhaled the last of the smoke. She tossed the butt on the ground and crushed it. I did the same with mine.

"I've already told you that I can't print any story you might give me," Natalie said. "Not here, not now. But I know there's a story, and I know it's the kind of story that a lot of people would like to read. You're just not telling me what it is."

I didn't want to make any promises, but I told her that if things worked out well, I'd tell her afterward.

"It might be too late by then. Reporters are arriving from all over the country to write about the race. They'll all have the same story that I do if you wait."

Nobody would have all of it. Nobody would know about Mitch, Givens, and Harry unless I told, and I didn't intend to. I might tell Natalie, though.

"There's a lot nobody will find out," I said. "They might get part of it, but they won't get all of it. I'll help you with that. What they find out will be just enough to get people interested. And you'll have the rest."

She looked at me thoughtfully, then said, "All right. I believe you."

I was glad to hear it, since I wasn't sure I even believed it myself.

TWENTY-FIVE

Tess had changed into jeans and a plaid shirt, with a Western hat and low-heeled boots. Sam's extra clothes were still back in the tent, so he was wearing his usual suit and bow tie. Not exactly the best outfit for a trip into the country, but it would have to do.

"What did you find out?" he wanted to know.

We were in the hotel lobby, where I'd met them after leaving the track. I told them about the note and what I'd learned from Natalie about Tres Robles. When she'd left the tent, I'd looked all around the track area for Amanda. I'd even asked Elizabeth Hawes and her mother if they'd seen her. Nobody had.

"Wilhelm has her," Sam said. "He must. He's going to kill her if you don't do what he wants."

"We don't know that," Tess said. "Why

don't we drive out to this Tres Robles ranch
and see what Harry has to say?"

I thought that was a good idea. Harry
hadn't said for me to come alone, any more
than he'd said what he wanted. But the "life
and death" comment to Boots implied that
it was important for me to talk to him. Like
Sam, I didn't think Harry was talking about
his own life. More than likely it was Amanda's. If it was, Harry was going to pay, one
way or another.

"You and Sam can ride in the buggy," I
told Tess. "I'll ride ahead on my horse."

"Do you know the way?"

I told her I did. I'd asked Natalie, and
she'd given me directions. It would be easy
to find.

"Let's go, then," Tess said.

Sam was about to jump out of his skin. I
hoped Tess could act as a calming influence
on him. If she didn't, he might leap out of
the buggy and run all the way to the old
ranch, which Natalie had told me was about
two miles out of town.

It would have been a pleasant ride under
other circumstances. Big white clouds
floated in the light blue sky, occasionally
obscuring the sun, and there was enough of
a breeze to keep me from being uncomfort-
ably warm. The countryside was green, and

the cayuse had an easy gait. But I couldn't stop thinking about Amanda and what I might find at the ranch house.

It sat on a low hill. The big oak that Natalie had told me about was at the foot of the hill beside a rutted road that hadn't seen much use lately. If five or six men joined hands, they might have been able to encircle the trunk of the tree, or the three trees. Some of the limbs were so long that they'd collapsed under their own weight and were touching the ground. Others were stretched out so far that I wondered why they hadn't drooped as well.

I reined in the cayuse and turned around in the saddle to see if the buggy was coming along. It was about a quarter of a mile behind. Tess was driving, or it might have passed me already. Sam might have worn out the whip.

I waited for them to catch up. When they had stopped beside me, Tess said, "What's the plan?"

I didn't have one, but I didn't think it would be a good idea to admit that. So I said, "I'll ride on up to the house and see what's going on. You follow me until you're about halfway there and wait."

"I don't want to wait," Sam said, straining forward on the seat. "Amanda might be up there."

"And she might not," I said. "We don't know what the situation is. So it's better to take our time and act carefully until we find out."

"He's right," Tess told Sam, putting a hand on his arm. "If we rush into things, we might be putting ourselves in danger. And others, too."

It was the "and others" that sold it. Tess was good at that sort of thing, much better than I was. Sam leaned back against the seat and let out a long, slow breath.

I left them there and rode up to the house. It was an old adobe building that hadn't been cared for in a long time. There was a bird's nest in one of the windows, and the front door was missing. Part of the roof had caved in. But I was betting that at least one big room on the inside had been made comfortable for Harry. He would have seen to that.

As I got to within about thirty yards of the place, Harry stepped out of the doorway. He was smiling, as he almost always was. The smile didn't mean anything. He'd been smiling the same way when he gut-shot the Mexicans.

The Winchester rifle he was holding meant a lot more. It was pointed straight at me.

"Hello, Dev," he said when I got closer.

"Hello, Harry. What's the life-and-death matter you wanted to see me about?"

He relaxed against the door frame, but the rifle didn't waver.

"You know what your problem is, Dev?"

"I know what several of them are. But I guess you're going to tell me what you think, anyway."

"Just as a personal favor. No criticism implied. But your problem is that you're too direct. You need to learn to ease into things, Dev. Give a fella time to catch his breath." He looked past me and back down the road. "Who's in the buggy?"

"My partners. No thanks to you, they're both with me again."

He smiled even more widely. "You know how it is, Dev. You have to work with what you've got, and Givens and Clarey were the best I could do. I needed a way to put some pressure on you, so I used your partner. I shouldn't have trusted Givens with the job of giving you the poison, though. That was a mistake. If I'd handled that little job, it might not have come down to this."

"What's it come down to?"

He made a slight motion with the rifle. "Better tell your partners not to come any farther. I'd hate to have to start shooting."

"You won't have to. They'll stop about halfway."

He waited and watched. I didn't look back, but I knew the buggy had stopped when his eyes focused on me again.

"I asked you what it's come down to," I said.

"See, that's what I mean. No time to talk with an old friend. Always rushing to the business at hand."

"You're not my friend, Harry. You never were."

Harry's smile dimmed, as if I'd hurt his feelings or disappointed him.

"I'm sorry you feel that way, Dev. I really am. After all, I was your partner once." He smiled again. "Those were the days, weren't they? We were young and full of piss and vinegar. The youngsters these days, they're not as smart as we were, are they?"

I didn't know what he meant by that, but I figured he'd tell me if I just kept quiet.

"The only person I see in that buggy is Miss O'Neill," he said. "That means somebody's trying to slip around and come up on me from the back way. I know you wouldn't try anything like that, Dev. You know better. So it was probably the kid's idea."

This time I did look back. Tess was coming slowly up the road, and she was the only one in the buggy. She was close enough for me to see the regretful look on her face.

I should have known that Sam would try something stupid and that Tess wouldn't be able to stop him. He'd been worked up already, and the thought that Amanda might be in the ranch house was too much for him. A more experienced operative would have known that talking to Harry was the best way to get Amanda back and that trying to fool him was the worst possible thing to do.

"Don't get excited, Dev," Harry said. "I can see you're itching to reach for that pistol as soon as I go inside to take care of your partner. But I'm not going inside. I'm not moving from right where I am."

"It doesn't matter," I said. "You must know by now that I'm not going to help you. You can kill Sam, and you can kill Amanda, too, but I'm not going to poison that horse."

The buggy stopped not far behind me. Tess didn't have anything to add to what I'd already said.

"I thought you might have a soft spot for the girl," Harry said. "But I should have known better. Nobody who works for the Boss has a soft spot for anybody."

Except Sam, I thought, but he was young. He'd learn. If he lived long enough.

"Why did you set all this up, Harry?" I said, hoping to give Sam some kind of chance. If I could keep Harry occupied, he wouldn't be able to deal with Sam. Not that he seemed interested in doing that.

"Money, Dev. It's always about money, isn't it? After the Boss set me loose, I managed to keep myself fed, but I could never get enough money together to live the way I wanted to. When I heard about this race and the size of the purse, I thought I'd found the answer to my problems. All I needed was somebody on the inside. And then I found out you'd be protecting the horse. That sounded like the perfect solution."

"How'd you find out about me?"

"That's my business. Let's just say I still have some friends in the old game. I'm sorry you aren't one of them."

If he'd really thought I was one of them, he'd have come to me and talked things over, tried to recruit me. I wondered who his informant was. Well, that was the Boss's problem now. He'd have to root out his own spies.

I heard a shot from the rear of the house, then another. Harry didn't move, just stood there relaxed against the door frame, the smile back on his face.

"You didn't think I was alone, did you, Dev? Givens and Clarey weren't the only ones working for me. We'll know in a minute whether the other man was any good or if your kid got the drop on him."

It didn't take even a minute. There was a sound behind Harry and he stepped out of the doorway. Sam came stumbling through it as if someone had shoved him. There was a dark stain on his right coat sleeve, and bright red drops of blood dripped off his fingers onto the ground.

He stopped short of the cayuse and looked up at me.

"I'm sorry, Dev." His face was twisted with pain. "I've let you down again."

"Don't worry about it, Sam."

"What will they do to Amanda?"

"Nothing."

I looked at the doorway, wondering who'd come through next. It was Rand, with his pistol drawn, with a smile wider than Harry's stretching his mouth. Now I knew why he'd been the one who wanted to beat some answers from Chip Briney. Harry couldn't afford to have anyone hurting Starcrossed. He wanted the horse to be in fine shape on the day of the race.

"Where do we go from here, Harry?" I

said, ignoring Rand.

"That's what I was going to ask you, Dev. If you don't care about the girl, maybe you care about the kid."

Rand thumbed back the hammer of his pistol, which was pointed right between Sam's shoulder blades.

Sam looked up at me. He knew what might be coming as well as I did. I couldn't meet his eyes.

"Just tell me one thing," I said to Harry. "Which horse were you betting on to win?"

"That's my little secret. One of many, I suppose. We've talked enough, Dev. Make up your mind. Are you with me or against me?"

All this time, Tess hadn't said a word. She sat in the buggy looking demure. She was good at that. Harry should have known she wasn't what she seemed, but he was so wrapped up in his schemes and with how clever he was that he hadn't watched her as closely as he should have been. I thought maybe I could distract him a little more.

"I'm against you, Harry. I guess I've been against you ever since you gut-shot those Mexicans."

Harry's smile disappeared completely. "Those greaser bastards killed my brother."

"Yeah. And he was just a kid. Like Sam, here."

"To hell with that. Sam works for the Boss. He knows what that means."

"What does it mean, Harry?"

"It means that he'd better be ready to die because you don't give a damn about him one way or the other. You'd rather stick up for what you like to think are principles than save his life. I'm tired of talking to you, Dev. I should have known you wouldn't cooperate. Now I'll have to find a way to get Rand close to that horse. It should be easy to do without you around."

"I'm not going anywhere."

"That's what you think. Kill the kid, Rand."

Twenty-Six

Rand didn't stand a chance. Tess shot him before he could pull the trigger, and he fell back through the door into the house.

I slid off the cayuse and grabbed at Sam's coat on the way down. I managed to get hold of his lapel and drag him to the ground with me as a bullet buzzed by my ear.

I heard Tess fire again, twice, while I was getting untangled from Sam and pulling the .44. Looking up, pistol in hand, I saw that Harry had ducked back into the house. He wouldn't show himself again until he thought he had an advantage, which wouldn't be too long, not if he had Amanda.

I stood up and said to Tess, "I was beginning to wonder if you'd thought to bring a gun."

"It was in my boot. I had a little trouble getting it out because your friend kept watching me."

"He's not my friend."

Sam got to his feet. His face was gray, and his wound was still bleeding.

"You'd better get in the buggy," I told him.

"He has Amanda in there," Sam said. "I saw her."

"We'll get her back. Don't worry."

"How?"

I wished he hadn't asked, because I didn't have an answer.

"We'll think of something, Sam," Tess said. "Get in the buggy."

He didn't want to do it, but he was hurting too much to argue. I thought his arm might be broken, the way it dangled at his side. Tess got down and we helped him into the buggy.

"Do you think you can drive it?" I said.

He grimaced and said, "I can do whatever I have to."

"Then go on down to the bottom of the hill. Tess and I will deal with Harry."

"Don't forget the other one."

"I won't."

I wasn't sure I had to worry much about Rand. Tess was a good shot.

Sam turned the buggy and drove away.

"Don't be too hard on him, Dev," Tess said. "He's young."

"He's too hotheaded. And I'm not sure he's tough enough to last long with the Boss."

"He might surprise you. And speaking of surprises, what do we do now?"

She reloaded her pistol with steady hands as she talked. She was the kind of professional I liked to work with.

"That's up to Harry," I said. "He'll most likely threaten us with killing Amanda next."

"Or he might just kill her."

She had a point. There was no telling what Harry might do now that he was riled up.

"You must know Harry better than I thought."

"I don't know him at all. But I've known men like him. Too many of them. If he hurts that girl . . ."

I took a glance down the hill. Sam had reached the bottom and turned the buggy around.

"I don't think Harry will kill Amanda, but if he does, he does. We can't give in to him. You know that."

"Knowing it doesn't mean I have to like it."

I might have gotten into a philosophical discussion with her, but Harry appeared at the door. Or rather Amanda did. Harry was standing behind her. Amanda's hands were behind her back, tied probably, and there was a gag tied around her mouth. Her eyes were wide, and I knew she must be scared. But she was trying not to show it.

"Last chance, Dev," Harry said. He was careful to keep himself hidden behind Amanda with his hand on her shoulder. "Either you do what I want, or I kill the girl."

"And then we kill you," I said.

"Maybe. Or maybe I'll kill you instead."

"There are two of us, Harry, and only one of you. Rand's out of it."

I wasn't sure about that. I just wanted to keep him talking, hoping that if I talked long enough, I'd think of something to do. So far, I hadn't.

Amanda had. She lifted her foot and brought it down on Harry's instep. He pulled the trigger of the rifle, but he was so startled by the sudden movement and the pain that he jerked the barrel to the side, and the bullet just grazed Amanda's side.

Amanda spun away from Harry and out the door. Both Tess and I fired into the house as soon as she was out of the way, but by then Harry was gone.

I started for the back of the house. Over my shoulder I yelled to Tess.

"If Harry comes out that door, kill him."

As if I needed to tell her that. I didn't bother to tell her to look after Amanda. I knew she'd do that, too.

Three horses stood in a little corral in back of the ranch house. It wasn't much of a corral. Some of the fence boards were missing, and others were rotted. It was partially shaded by a big oak.

Harry was halfway out the back door. I took a quick shot at him before he saw me. The bullet chipped a chunk of adobe from the wall, and dust flew.

Harry kept coming. I wasn't expecting that, and my next shot was way off target. It knocked the heel off one of his boots, and then he was behind the oak.

He had the advantage on me, so I moved around to the side of the house. I took a look around the corner, but I couldn't see Harry.

I did see Rand. He hobbled out the back door, bent over and wheezing like a locomotive. Tess's bullet must have clipped a lung.

"Hold it, Rand," I said. "Go on back inside."

He turned in my direction, but I was mostly hidden behind the wall, and I don't think he saw me. I moved so that he could.

"Go to hell, Mallory," he said, his breath rasping in and out.

Harry must have thought all my attention was on Rand. He took the opportunity to slide around the oak and take a shot at me. He missed, but he scared Rand, who brought up his pistol. I shot him in the head, and he fell backward.

Harry fired again, but I was behind the wall. Flakes of adobe spatted my face as the bullet took off part of the corner of the house.

I was about to take another look when I heard Tess say, "Drop the rifle, Harry, and turn around very slowly."

"Now why would I want to do that?" Harry said.

Tess didn't know Harry as well as I did. He'd never drop the rifle, even if she'd sneaked up behind him. He wouldn't believe she'd shoot him.

I rounded the corner of the house as Harry was turning and bringing the rifle to bear on Tess.

He didn't have a prayer. Tess shot him twice, then shot him a third time as he crumpled to his knees.

Harry got off one shot, but it went into the ground. He balanced on his knees, bent forward until his head touched the ground. He balanced like that for a couple of seconds, then fell to the side.

I went over to have a look at him. Tess was already standing over him.

"I guess you win, Dev," Harry said.

He was looking up at me, but I don't think he saw me. I don't think he saw anything. There was a good bit of blood on his chest. Tess had hit him with every shot.

"I wouldn't call it winning," I said.

"I won't be needing the money now," he said. "You can use that poison yourself, Dev. Get rich."

"You know better than that."

"Yeah, I guess I do. Too bad about those principles of yours. You have a good partner, though."

Tess stood there reloading her pistol and didn't say anything.

"She's the best," I said, but Harry didn't hear me.

He shuddered and a little blood ran out of his mouth, and that was all.

"I had to do it," Tess said.

Maybe she'd known Harry wouldn't drop the rifle, after all. "And you wanted to," I said.

I wasn't accusing her. I didn't even blame her.

"He's the one responsible for what Givens and Clarey did to me. You killed Givens, so there wasn't anybody left for me to kill except this one."

I nudged Harry with my toe. He didn't

move. I supposed I'd have to tell Rossiter. He wasn't going to like it. But somebody would have to send an undertaker out for Harry and Rand. That would be Rossiter's job.

"How's Amanda?"

"Just a scratch. She'll be all right. I sent her down the road to see about Sam."

"He'll thank you for that."

Tess put her hand on my arm. "It's not over, is it?" she said.

"No. We still don't know who's trying to stop Starcrossed from running in the race."

"Then it's time we figured that out."

"Yeah," I said. "It sure is."

Rossiter was upset, but there was nothing he could do. I was federal law, and he was local, so I had the upper hand. After he calmed down, he agreed to send someone for the bodies.

We took Sam to the doctor, who said he thought he'd just drop all his other patients and follow me around. He'd have plenty of work that way.

Amanda said she'd stay with Sam until his arm was taken care of and then drive him back to the track. They'd ridden back to town in the buggy and gotten better acquainted. Sam's noble suffering and the fact that he'd been shot trying to save her must have impressed her, I thought.

Tess and I went back to her room at the hotel. I needed a drink and a smoke. She didn't have a bottle, but the desk clerk had one sent up.

I felt tired and old. Maybe it was the way Harry had died. He'd never been worth a damn, but I hated to see him go like that. It seemed like a waste, somehow.

After we'd both had a drink and I'd smoked two cigarettes, Tess said, "Have you figured it out yet?"

"Somebody's trying to stop Starcrossed. I have an idea, but I'm not sure what the reason might be."

"Amateurs," Tess said. "Judging from what you've told me, I'd say they don't know what they're doing."

She had a good point, and it fit with what I'd been thinking.

"Harry knew what he was doing," she went on. "He just picked the wrong person to do it. He should have joined forces with the others."

"He didn't know who they were. Rand tried to beat it out of Chip Briney, but he wouldn't tell. He'd given his sacred word."

"And then he died before you could put any more pressure on him."

"That's right. But I don't know who killed him, or even how. He just died."

Even as I was talking, I thought of something that someone had said. I'd thought nothing of it at the time, but it fit in with everything else that had been going on.

"I have to talk to Rossiter," I said.

"You think Rossiter did it?"

"No, but I think he can tell me who did. I'm going to the jail."

"Me, too," Tess said.

TWENTY-SEVEN

Rossiter was sitting in his usual spot. He didn't even move when we rode up, not to greet me, not out of politeness to Tess.

We dismounted and walked up to where he sat.

"I have a question for you," I said.

"Ask it. Maybe I'll answer."

"You don't have to be a horse's ass, Rossiter. I didn't call you in about Harry because I had to deal with him myself."

"Yeah. You killed him."

I hadn't killed him, but I let it pass.

"Here's the question. Did Chip Briney have any visitors before he died?"

"He might have."

"Clarey tells me you serve a good breakfast. Did Briney's visitors come while he was eating?"

"What if they did?"

"I think he was poisoned."

I told Rossiter about Sterling. He leaned

forward, and the chair's legs thunked down. He pushed back his hat and gave me a direct look.

"Who'd do a thing like that?"

"I'm not sure. That's why I'm asking about Briney's visitors."

"Two women," Rossiter said. "Good-looking ones."

Elizabeth and Davinia Hawes. I should have thought about them sooner. Liz was exactly the kind of person to whom Chip would have given his "sacred word." I wondered about the death of Mr. Hawes. Had he died the same way Chip Briney had?

"You think they poisoned that kid?" Rossiter said.

"They might have. Now I have to prove it."

"That's my job. He was my prisoner."

"You can come along. Get your horse."

Rossiter crabbed away. Tess said, "He's not going to be any help. A hindrance, more like."

"You're going to have to keep him out of the way."

"How am I supposed to do that?"

"You'll think of something," I said.

Motive, that was the thing I was missing. Liz Hawes wanted to marry Prince John, not destroy him, or so I thought. And I couldn't figure how Liz could have gotten into the stable to make the attempt on Star-crossed the morning that Jake had calmed him. Or how she'd shot me. She didn't seem like the type to use a gun. An Englishwoman and poison, that I could understand. But not a gun. It just didn't seem to fit with her methods.

When we got back to the track, I asked Tess to take Rossiter for some lemonade while I checked to see if Sam had returned and what the doc had said about his arm.

As I'd expected, Rossiter didn't object to spending some time in Tess's company. They went off for the lemonade, and I went to my tent.

Sam was there, lying on the cot. Amanda sat on my cot, watching him. She looked up when I came inside.

"Dev," she said, "I don't think I've properly thanked you for saving me from Harry. I thought he was nice, but I was wrong. He was horrible."

"I didn't save you," I said, looking over at the cot. "It was all Sam's doing."

Sam gave me a weak grin.

"He's the one who figured the whole thing out," I continued. "He risked his life coming around the back way to get you out of that place. He's lucky Rand didn't kill him."

"I was just stupid," Sam said. "Stupid and impulsive."

"You were not!" Amanda told him. "Don't ever say that about yourself."

"Well, I guess it was kind of heroic, when you think about it," Sam said. "And I did get shot."

"You certainly did." Amanda moved over to sit on the edge of his cot. She looked back at me. "His arm's broken. He's not going to be much help to you, but I can take care of him."

"What about Starcrossed?"

"The prince can always find somebody to help with that horse. He doesn't need me."

The prince. Not *John.* I had a feeling that Amanda was over her crush on him. She'd found somebody who liked her and needed her and who wasn't weepy-eyed all the time. Sam was a lucky young man. I wondered how Richard Caldwell would take it.

And then I wondered something else.

First I had a talk with Tess and Rossiter, and then I sent word to Liz Hawes and her mother that I'd like for them to join us for lemonade. It was late afternoon, and there were very few people still at the track. Tomorrow morning they would be there early to see the rodeo and they would all stay for the race in the afternoon, when they'd be joined by many others. But now the track area was fairly quiet.

I wasn't sure that the Haweses would come, but they did. The messenger I'd sent had been persuasive, I was sure. He came along with them.

Richard Caldwell.

"I don't understand why you have asked us to come here," Mrs. Hawes said after everyone was seated at the table. "It's an interruption of my afternoon's activities."

"High tea?" I asked.

She glared at me. So did Liz. Two statues carved out of cold stone by the same sculptor.

I got lemonade for them and for Richard and was careful to give them their glasses myself. Tess and Rossiter had theirs already.

"Now," I said, sitting at the table with a lemonade of my own, "it's time we all had a talk."

"I don't see the need for that," Liz said, and her mother nodded. "We have nothing to discuss."

Her tone indicated that she felt we were too far below her to know anything that might interest her. But I had other ideas.

"We can talk about why you had me shot,"

I said. "And about why you killed Chip Briney."

Neither Liz nor her mother batted an eye. Liz took a sip of her lemonade and said, "Who?"

"It won't work," I said. "You're very good, but it won't work. The marshal here knows you were at the jail, and I know you poisoned Chip's food."

"You know nothing of the sort," Mrs. Hawes said.

"I think you poisoned your late husband, too," I told her.

She turned her frosty eyes on me. "You forget yourself, Mr. Mallory." She rose from her chair. "Come, Elizabeth. We're leaving."

"That wouldn't be a good idea," Tess said.

"And why not?"

"Because I think Dev poisoned your lemonade."

Twenty-Eight

Tess's remark got more of a reaction than anything I'd said. The two women were thunderstruck. I'd never seen them have much of a reaction to anything before, but this time their eyes widened, and Mrs. Hawes actually gaped, though not for long.

Beside me, Richard jumped up, his chair tumbling back behind him

Rossiter said, "You'd better be joking about that, Miss O'Neill."

She smiled a demure smile. "You can call me Tess."

I took the vial out of my pocket and held it up for all of them to see.

"A man named Harry Wilhelm wanted me to give the liquid in this container to Starcrossed. That didn't work out, but I thought it might be interesting to see if it works on humans."

Liz Hawes gasped.

Richard stood rigidly, his hands at his

sides. He took rapid breaths through his open mouth.

"I didn't give you much," I told Liz. "Not as big a dose as whatever you gave Donald Sterling, and you haven't even drunk all your lemonade. The doctor can fix you right up with a purge. That is, if I let you see him."

I put the vial in my pocket, drew my .44, and laid it on the table in front of me as if to threaten them further.

"You can't do this, Mallory," Rossiter said. "It's murder."

"It's only murder if they die," I said as if it didn't matter to me one way or the other. "They might, but I don't think they will. If they do, it's no more than they deserve. They tried to kill Starcrossed. They did kill Jake Duncan."

"We had nothing to do with that man's death," Mrs. Hawes said. She had recovered her usual icy equanimity. She seemed perfectly calm, as if she didn't care one way or the other about being poisoned. "We were nowhere near those stables when the fire started or when you were shot."

"I believe you," I said. "You couldn't have done it alone. You had to have help. That's why you got Chip Briney involved. Chip was just an inexperienced kid. A woman like Liz could twist him around her finger and get him to do just about anything. She could persuade him to give his sacred word not to involve her, no matter what. You thought you'd be all right until he got tossed in Rossiter's jail. He was scared, and you didn't have any way to control him there, so he had to be put out of the way."

"You don't know what you're saying," Liz told me. "Please, get us to a doctor."

"*Please.* That's very good, Liz, but maybe later. After you've told me what I want to know."

"We will tell you nothing," Mrs. Hawes said, but I thought she was turning a little pale.

So was Liz. The color had drained from her face, and she looked unsteady, as if she might fall off her chair. I couldn't see Richard, but I could hear his ragged breathing. I could feel him twitching beside me.

"We couldn't possibly have done what you think," Mrs. Hawes said. "You can't truly believe that we did."

"Like I said, I don't believe you did it all yourselves. I think you had Chip Briney's help."

"He couldn't have shot you. He was apprehended after setting the fire."

"I know." I took out the vial again, held it

up, and jiggled it. "That's why I poisoned Richard's lemonade, too."

Richard let out a yell and made a dive for my pistol. He was overweight and clumsy, and I think he was surprised that he actually got to it before I did. He jerked it up from the table and backed away, waving the barrel back and forth between me and Rossiter. He was ignoring Tess, which could have been a mistake under other circumstances.

"I'm going to the doctor," he said. "Don't try to stop me."

"It won't help," I said. "I gave you more than the others because you're the one who shot me."

"And I'll do it again, you bastard."

Richard thumbed back the hammer and pulled the trigger. There was a click, but that was all, since I'd taken the precaution of unloading the pistol.

Rossiter's pistol was loaded, however, and he drew it as he stood up.

"Drop the gun, son," he told Richard.

Richard looked as if he might break into tears. He didn't want to drop the gun. Maybe he still couldn't quite believe it wouldn't shoot. He tried it again with the same result as before, and I got up and took it out of his limp hand.

"Have a seat, Richard," I said, "and tell us all about it."

It took him a while, but what it boiled down to was this: Richard had been jealous of Prince John for a long time, and John's seemingly easy conquest of Amanda after Richard had fallen in love with her was just too much. Richard was willing to do almost anything to see John take a tumble, and while he didn't think he could handle John, Starcrossed was a different story.

According to Richard, Liz Hawes was upset with John's attitude toward her. The prince was supposed to become infatuated with her, as most men did, and marry her. It seems that the family fortune that Liz and her mother had inherited upon Mr. Hawes's convenient death was running out, and they needed a new source of income. Prince John was chosen, but he'd proved tougher to convince than they'd thought he would be. And then Amanda had shown up, making things even more difficult for them.

"So they decided to cause problems," Richard said, sitting with his hands clasped in front of him on the table. He kept his eyes down, not looking at anyone. "They thought that John would realize he needed a steady British woman at his side in times of trouble, and not some American tramp, especially if her father could be blamed for the trouble."

The Hawes women looked at Richard with as much contempt as they could muster while he told his story. They weren't feeling well enough to give him the full treatment. For that matter, Richard wasn't feeling too well himself.

"I didn't like what they said about Amanda," he went on. He gagged a couple of times, but nothing was expelled. He recovered and continued. "When they asked me to help, I was willing. I thought I might be the one Amanda would turn to when John preferred Liz."

It hadn't worked out like that at all. John remained indifferent to both women, and Amanda had shown no interest in Richard.

"I'm the one who shot you," Richard told me. "I was watching the fire, and I thought you were going into the stable to save Starcrossed. I didn't know Amanda's father was in there, I swear it. I'd give anything to take back what happened."

It was too late for that now. I said, "Did you have anything to do with the poisoning of Sterling and Briney?"

"No. I'm the one who got into the stable and fixed it so Starcrossed would go wild that morning, but that's all I did. I had a badge. Everyone trusted me."

I didn't say what a mistake that had been. I asked him what he'd done to Starcrossed.

"After the groom had picked his feet, I went in to see him. He knew me, so I didn't have any trouble with him. I slipped a sharp stone in the hoof, so that it would touch the frog. Starcrossed has his feet picked every day before he goes out and every day when he comes in. So he's never felt any pain there before. I tried to place the stone so it would stab the frog, not at first, but after it moved a bit."

"Why didn't the groom find it later?"

"Starcrossed was too upset. They didn't pick his feet until that evening. Mr. Duncan was the one who did it."

And there it was, the thing that would hang Richard, if a member of the gentry could be hanged in this country. I said, "How did you know that?"

Richard's head jerked up, and he looked at me. I saw dismay and despair in his eyes, in equal amounts.

"You knew he'd check," I said. "You stopped him."

Richard looked down again. "Yes. I hit him while he was bent over, looking at the hoof. Then I ran. I didn't know that anyone was going to burn the stable. I didn't know."

Maybe he hadn't known about the fire, and maybe he hadn't known that Jake was still inside when the fire started. But he'd made sure I wouldn't get into the stable. I wouldn't shed any tears when he went up the gallows. Neither would Amanda.

"I think that's all," I told Rossiter. "You can make your arrests now."

"What about the doctor?" Liz said. "We need treatment."

"He didn't really poison the lemonade," Tess said. "This was all a play."

We'd set it up beforehand. Rossiter had been in on it, of course. He'd played his part better than I'd thought he would.

"So you haven't really been poisoned," Tess said to everyone.

I shook my head. "Oh, yes, they have."

Even Tess was shocked. But I let them know that what they'd drunk wasn't really poison, not strictly.

I'd slipped a small dose of an emetic into the lemonade I'd given the Hawes women and Richard. It wasn't enough to hurt them, but it was enough to make them plenty uncomfortable, which is all I'd wanted. I didn't tell anyone that, however. If they thought they might die, so much the better.

I let Rossiter take them to the doctor. Hell, a purge would do them good, even though it wouldn't purge them of the kind of sickness that had made them do the things they'd done to Starcrossed, to Sterling, to Jake. And to Chip Briney.

Chip's death was a sticking point. So was Sterling's near death, for that matter. It didn't make much difference what Richard said about the Hawes women. I didn't think they'd ever confess to anything, and there was no way to prove they'd poisoned either Sterling or Chip. It was just Richard's word against theirs, and they would be far more formidable than Richard ever would if the case ever came to court. I doubted that it would. Chip was dead, so he couldn't testify against them. Richard was weak, and he'd suffer the consequences. Liz and Davinia Hawes would slip the noose and go their frigid way, conniving against some other man now that their hopes for having Liz marry John had fallen apart.

It was a disappointing outcome. Rossiter arrested both women, but the woman lawyer that Rossiter had mentioned to Chip Briney had them out of jail within an hour. They didn't even have to spend the night.

Their standing with John would never recover, but then it hadn't been very high to begin with. The only good thing to come out of the whole mess was the introduction of Sam to Amanda.

When I got back to the tent, things between those two were going just fine. Sam was able to comfort Amanda when I told them what Richard had done and how he was responsible for Jake's death. I left them and went to Tess's hotel to have something to eat. I figured they'd have plenty more to say to each other that evening, and they wouldn't want me around to hear it.

And that was how things would have ended if Chance Oliver hadn't gotten his ribs kicked in.

Twenty-Nine

Chance Oliver was the jockey who'd be riding Starcrossed in the race. Or he would have been.

I wasn't there when the fight started. I'd stayed awhile at the hotel and talked things over with Tess after we'd eaten, and then I'd come back to the track. I was headed for my tent when I heard the ruckus, and by the time I got to the cowboys' bunkhouse, the fight was well under way.

Boots Donovan was part of the group that ringed the two men who were whaling away at each other. I touched his arm to get his attention and asked what was going on.

"One of them jockeys got into it with Stick Walters," he said. "I don't know what the argument was about, but it's getting settled now."

As he said that, I saw Walters knock the other man, whom I recognized as Oliver, to the ground. Walters could have left it at that, but he started kicking the jockey, making sure that the toe of his boot came into contact with the smaller man's ribs.

I shoved through the crowd and grabbed Walters's shoulder, spinning him around.

That was a mistake. Walters's blood was up, and he wasn't in any mood to be hindered in what he was doing. His big, hard right fist slammed into the side of my head like a piece of lumber and knocked me flat. I hadn't even seen it coming.

I lay still for a couple of seconds, then pushed myself up and shook my head to clear it. Shaking just made things worse, and I stayed where I was, braced on my arms. Off to the side, Walters was kicking Oliver again.

Boots came over and helped me to my feet. I didn't shake my head this time. I pulled the .44.

"Jesus, Dev," Boots said.

He must have thought I was going to shoot Walters, and I won't say the thought didn't cross my mind. But I didn't shoot him. I fired a couple of bullets into the side of the bunkhouse to get his attention.

He turned to face me, his eyes burning. He was ready to swing on me again, but the sight of the big pistol discouraged him.

"Get away from Oliver," I said.

Walters didn't say a word. He just stood there, breathing through his mouth.

"Take him aside, Boots," I said. I could feel my finger tighten on the trigger. "Before I shoot him."

Boots went over to Walters and took his arm. Walters shook him off and glared at me. I figured I was going to have to shoot him, after all, and I wouldn't mind a bit.

But his eyes started to clear. He looked down at Oliver, who wasn't moving, and said, "Little bastard called me a son of a bitch. He didn't have any reason. Just walked up to me and said it. I don't take that kinda talk from nobody."

Walters was a hothead. All the cowboys knew about his temper. So did everyone else, and I couldn't figure out why Oliver would have done something so stupid, especially the day before he was supposed to ride Starcrossed.

"Stick's telling the truth," one of the cowboys said. "I was here. We were just having ourselves a smoke, and that fella came up to Stick and cussed him. I don't blame Stick for what he did."

Nobody else blamed him, either, not even me, though I thought his reaction had been a little bit excessive. I told Stick to get out of the bunkhouse and holstered my pistol.

Boots and I checked Oliver as the crowd started to break up. The jockey was barely conscious, and all he could do was moan. I knew then that he wouldn't be riding in the race the next day, and from what I'd heard nobody else was capable of doing the job, not the right way.

Harry would have had a good laugh about that if he'd been there, I was sure.

"Who's gonna tell the prince?" Boots said.

"I will, if you'll get Oliver over to the jockeys' quarters. Get somebody to help you. And get the doctor."

I thought that I should ask the doc for a percentage of his take. His business had picked up a lot since I'd come to town.

John wasn't as upset as I'd thought he might be. Or maybe that's the way princes are, calm in the face of impending disaster. I didn't know, not having been around that many princes.

He and Steffens met me in the parlor of Steffens's house. They told me that Sterling was asleep upstairs. He was going to be all right, but he wouldn't be able to work with Starcrossed for a while.

"But that won't matter," John said. "The race is tomorrow. The time for working with the horse is done. He's ready for the race, and now is the time for him to prove himself again. And I have no doubt that he will."

"But who'll be the rider?" Steffens asked. "Oliver's the best, and he knows the horse. Nobody else will do."

John said that wasn't the case. "Miss Duncan might suit just fine."

Steffens's face changed. He looked the way Liz did when she thought she was poisoned. He said, "A woman?"

John nodded and looked at me. I knew that Amanda could ride, and so did Steffens. That wasn't what he was worried about.

"You have a woman lawyer here in town," I said, "and you have a woman reporter. Why not a woman jockey?"

His face changed again. He looked like a man who'd just swallowed his chaw.

"It's just not right."

"Be that as it may," John said, "it's the best chance we have."

Steffens mulled it over for a few seconds. Then he said, "And if she loses?"

"That will be all right, since no one will expect her to win. It's a long chance, but it's our only one. But think of this: As soon as people find out that she's riding, the odds will turn against Starcrossed. What if he wins? We'll make even more money."

Steffens brightened a little at that. "You think it's possible?"

John shrugged. "She knows the horse, and the horse knows her. What other choice do we have?"

"Well, it's your horse. And I certainly don't want to pull him from the race, or cancel it."

John looked at me. "Will you ask her, Dev?"

"Sure," I said.

I went by the jockeys' quarters on the way to the tent. The place smelled of saddle leather, liniment, and sweat. Oliver was lying on his bunk. The doctor had finished taping him up and was about to leave. I told him my idea of working on a percentage.

"You might think that's funny, but I don't think that fella on the bunk does." He gestured at Oliver. "You're a jinx if there ever was one."

"I like to think some things that happen aren't my fault."

"You keep on thinking like that. Maybe you'll sleep better."

He snapped his black medical bag shut and left without saying anything more. I decided that he didn't have a sense of humor.

Oliver didn't feel much like talking, but I had a question for him anyway.

"Why did you go after Stick Walters, Chance? You know what that temper of his is like."

Oliver raised his head to look at me, then lay back and closed his eyes.

"I had to brace him. He said some things about me."

"What things?"

"Things he shouldn't have said. About me and horses. And what I did to them."

I told him I didn't understand.

"He said I liked them the way he likes women."

"He said that to your face?"

"No. He was too much of a coward for that. Somebody told me about it."

I had a feeling that I might know the parties in question. "Who?"

"I can't tell you that. I promised I wouldn't."

"Gave your sacred word, I'm sure."

"Wasn't anything said about *sacred*."

The Hawes women hadn't been out of jail more than an hour or so. They hadn't wasted any time.

"I can't do it," Amanda said.

"Yes, you can," I told her.

320

Sam added his encouragement. She was still sitting on the side of his cot when I'd returned to the tent. I'd made one stop first, but Liz Hawes and her mother weren't in their room. That was fine with me. I'd paid the room a visit anyway.

"Jake would be proud," I told Amanda. It was a cheap ploy, but I thought it might work. "It's what he'd want you to do. If you don't, then Liz and Davinia are going to be the winners."

Amanda lifted her chin. "I don't want them to win anything."

"They're operating out of sheer spite now," I said. "They know they'll never have John, so they don't want Starcrossed to win. They're the ones who got Oliver into that fight."

That cinched it.

"Starcrossed will win the race," Amanda said. "I'll see to that."

I didn't doubt it.

THIRTY

The next day was clear and sunny. Women carrying colorful parasols and men wearing wide-brimmed hats watched the rodeo and responded with laughter and applause to the rope twirling, the trick riding, and the shooting of the tossed wooden blocks.

Some of the crowd might even have thought they were getting a true idea of what cowboys did on a working ranch. Everybody else knew it was just a show.

But it was a good show, and Boots Donovan was one of the stars. From the back of his galloping horse, he shot at and broke six glass balls suspended on strings. Then he stood up on the saddle and waved his hat to the crowd.

"He's quite something, isn't he?" Natalie Davis said.

Tess and I agreed. We had to raise our voices a little to be heard because of the hum of all the other conversations going on

322

around us and the shouting of the vendors.

We were seated with Natalie in the grandstand, and like everyone else we were waiting for the main event. The rodeo was exciting and entertaining, but it wasn't what had brought the people who crowded the grandstand and lined the rail. The race was what mattered, and because many people had heard about the woman rider, it had become even more important.

"When are you going to tell me the rest of your interesting story?" Natalie asked. "You promised, remember?"

"You know most of it now," I said. "You've talked to Rossiter, haven't you?"

"Yes, but so has every other reporter in town."

"You'll get a few more good paragraphs when Amanda wins the race."

"And so will all the others. You know things that nobody else does. I want to hear them."

"You might as well tell her," Tess said. "It doesn't matter now."

The race wouldn't begin for another hour or more, so I said that we'd better leave the stands. I didn't want anybody overhearing what I had to say.

We went to my tent. Sam wasn't there. His arm was still hurting, but he wanted to be with Amanda at the stables.

I told Natalie most of what had happened, starting with Tess's abduction but omitting that I'd known Harry in the past and leaving out the fact that he'd worked for the government. Natalie didn't ask how he'd known we were on the train. If it occurred to her later, I didn't plan to answer.

When I was finished, Natalie said to Tess, "I'm glad you shot Wilhelm."

Tess just nodded.

"And no one else knows all this?" Natalie said.

"You're the only one," I said. "You can tell the story, but you can't use our names."

She agreed without argument.

"And I can't print the part about those two women," she said. "There's no proof of their involvement, and they're not in jail."

"That's right. But maybe that story isn't over yet."

"What do you mean?"

"I mean that they might get in more trouble. But that's just something you'll have to wait and see."

"We'd better get back to the track," Tess said. "It's almost time for the race."

None of us wanted to miss that.

I'd been invited by Prince John to sit in his

box for the race itself, and he was happy to include Tess and Natalie in the invitation. There was no sign of Liz and Davinia Hawes, which wasn't surprising. I supposed they'd been forced to sit in the stands with the common folk, where they'd be cheering for Amanda to break her neck. That is, if they ever did anything so vulgar as cheering.

The prince wasn't as happy a man as you'd think he'd be on the big day. But he had a lot on his mind. His cousin, Richard, was in jail, charged with murder. His jockey had broken ribs and was lying on a cot, pretty much helpless, leaving the race in the hands of a young, inexperienced rider. For all that, he was calm and self-possessed.

Carter Steffens was in the box, too. He tried to put on a jovial front, but I could tell that he was nervous. He pulled out one of his big cigars.

"I hope you ladies don't mind if I smoke," he said to Tess and Natalie.

No one objected, so he lit up and smoke wreathed his head. I'd always liked the smell of burning cigars, though I didn't like to smoke them.

The bugler sounded first call, and the horses came out to the track to line up for the start. Some of the jockeys were accompanied by trainers, who walked alongside the horses, giving last-minute advice and reviewing the strategy for the race.

No trainer was near Amanda. She was trainer and jockey all in one, and I hoped she was up to the job. She'd told me that morning that she wasn't worried, but I didn't think that was true. Anybody in her position would have been worried. I'd have been scared stupid.

I looked down at the track. They were getting the horses in position at the starting line. Starcrossed looked calm. Some of the other horses were nervous, shying to the side, turning to bite their riders, kicking.

"That's Wonderment trying to bite," Steffens said. "He's got plenty of gumption."

"I don't think gumption matters at the starting line," John said. "It's only later that it counts, during the race. Look at Miss Duncan. She seems to have Starcrossed in fine fettle."

I agreed. And I didn't think Wonderment would win. If I'd been betting, I'd have put my money on Amanda and Starcrossed. I took up a pair of field glasses and looked at Amanda. She seemed as calm as Starcrossed, purposeful, ready to go.

I looked for Sam and spotted him at the railing. He could have been in the box with us, but he wanted to be as close to Amanda as possible.

Eventually the horses were all lined up. There was still a little jostling going on, but not enough to cause problems, I hoped.

I'd heard that back East they were using a bell to start races, and that's what they planned to use today here in Corvair. I waited for the sound, and then it came, pealing loud and clear. When it did, the horses surged away from the starting line like a brown ocean wave.

It was an amazing sight to see those animals run, all that power and speed, and it was being controlled by the jockeys who weren't a tenth the size of the horses. Dirt flew up from under the hooves as the horses ran. The jockeys sat upright, holding the reins and urging the big animals on. Some of them were already using their whips.

Not Amanda. Through the field glasses I could see the tension and excitement on her face. And a wide grin that stretched her mouth.

Wonderment and Belle, Ellie Vernon's horse, were in front, running neck and neck, and by the first turn they were a full length in front of the only horse close to them, a bay named Stonewall.

Tess leaned forward, her eyes riveted on

the horses. She'd never seen a race before, and she was completely caught up in the drama.

"What's wrong with Starcrossed?" Natalie said. "Why is he so far behind?"

"He's waiting for his chance," I said, hoping I knew what I was talking about. I glanced at Steffens and the prince for confirmation, but they were concentrating on the horses and had nothing to say.

Amanda still didn't use the whip. A horse tried to pass her on the rail, and Starcrossed sped up. It was as if he'd received some kind of unheard command, and the other horse dropped back. But there was still a wall of horses between Starcrossed and the other leaders, and I wondered how Amanda would possibly get through.

"That isn't fair!" Natalie said. "They're deliberately blocking her!"

I didn't know if that was true or not, but it could have been. There had been quite a bit of dissension when the prince had announced that a woman would be riding Starcrossed. It wouldn't have been surprising if the jockeys had united to be sure she didn't win.

Before I could say any of that, a little gap opened between two of the horses. It didn't seem big enough to me, but it must have looked just fine to Amanda and Starcrossed, who put on another burst of speed and slipped through the gap almost before I had a chance to register what he was doing.

Then he was in the clear and there were only three horses in front of him: Wonderment, Belle, and Stonewall, still trailing the others by a length.

Starcrossed took the rail to pass Stonewall as they reached the end of the backstretch. There was plenty of room, but Stonewall lunged sideways as Starcrossed started by and bumped him. I wasn't sure about the earlier blocking, but the bump had to be deliberate.

Steffens nearly bit his cigar in two. The prince clenched his fists and his teeth. His mouth was a thin line.

Starcrossed's front legs buckled, and I was sure he was going down. But he didn't. Amanda kept his head up. He ran awkwardly for several steps while Amanda steadied him, and as they rounded the final curve he was running free and fast again. And again he took the rail.

"If that son of a bitch bumps Starcrossed again, he'll never ride in another race," Steffens said.

As Starcrossed started to pass, Stonewall again tried to crowd him. But this time

Amanda was ready. She didn't use the whip. She leaned forward the way Jake had and seemed to whisper in the horse's ear, and Starcrossed shot past Stonewall as if the other horse were standing still.

Starcrossed had lost a bit of ground, but he flew down the homestretch with Amanda leaning forward, still talking to him, and he passed Wonderment and Belle before the finish line, winning the race by half a length.

The grandstand was a tumult of shouting and cheering and people slapping each other on the back. Those who'd bet on Starcrossed were happy. I swept the field glasses over the crowd to see if I could catch sight of Liz Hawes, but I couldn't.

Tess and Natalie had both jumped to their feet almost at the beginning of the race. They sat down and leaned back in their chairs.

"My, my," Tess said.

"My, my, indeed," Natalie said.

Steffens was more vocal. "I've never seen a ride like it. I don't give a good goddamn if she is a woman. Amanda Duncan can ride a goddamn horse."

The prince seemed a little embarrassed at such language in front of ladies, though I suspected that neither Tess nor Natalie really qualified in that regard.

"She won," he said, as if he'd never really believed it would happen, in spite of his choice of Amanda as his rider. "We should go down and celebrate."

Nobody gave him an argument.

Amanda and Starcrossed were surrounded by well-wishers, a group that did not include Liz and Davinia Hawes. Just about everyone else was there. Boots and the cowboys, the trainers, the grooms, and what seemed like half the crowd from the grandstands.

And right beside her, one hand on Starcrossed's bridle, was Sam. I don't know who looked happier, Sam or Amanda. I wished that Jake could have been there.

Prince John treated us to a big dinner that night at Steffens's house. Somehow Natalie Davis had wangled an invitation and brought Boots along. I'd never seen him dressed in anything other than his cowboy duds, and in a suit he looked as uncomfortable as a virgin in a whorehouse.

Amanda was the center of attention, but she had eyes only for Sam. The way those two had hit it off was a source of amazement to me, but I was happy for them. The Boss didn't like to have married men on his payroll, and I thought that was just as well for Sam. He was game, but he wasn't cut out for the work, and he'd be happier doing something else.

After dinner, the men went to the library for cigars and brandy, but I didn't join them. I had somewhere else I wanted to be.

Tess, who knew where I was headed, came with me. We hadn't gotten far before Natalie Davis caught up with us.

"Where are you two off to?" she said.

"The railroad station." I looked at my watch. "Last train leaves town in fifteen minutes."

"And you're planning to be on it?"

"No, but I think I know who is."

"I'm going with you," Natalie said.

I looked at Tess, who said, "Why not? She needs an ending for her story."

"What about Boots?" I said.

Natalie smiled. "He's in the library, swelling around with the other men."

"All right. Come on along."

We got out of the buggy and went into the depot. I saw Marshal Rossiter just as he accosted Liz and Davinia Hawes, who were about to step out onto the boarding platform. We started in that direction.

"You have no reason to accost us," Davinia said. "Leave us alone."

"I apologize, ma'am," Rossiter said, not sounding apologetic at all. "But I have to do this."

"Do what?" Liz said. "If we miss our train, you're going to be sorry."

She was carrying her reticule and a small valise. Rossiter reached out and took the valise from her.

"Give that back," Davinia said. "It's not your property."

Rossiter didn't say anything. He walked to a bench and set the valise down, opened it, and began looking through it. It didn't take him long to find what he was looking for. He brought it out of the valise and held it up. It was the vial I'd gotten from Givens.

"Looks mighty suspicious to me," Rossiter said. "Could be poison."

"I don't know how that got in there," Liz said. "It doesn't belong to me." Then she saw Tess and me. "They're the ones who put it there. You saw it in his hand yesterday, and you know it."

"Don't know anything of the kind," Rossiter said. "Now Mr. Sterling is still alive, and I don't suppose he's about to die, but he was poisoned for sure. The doc said so, and I believe him. Could be this is what did it. We'll have to get it analyzed, and after that we'll see what happens. Until then, you two ladies will have to be my guests in the jail."

Davinia stepped up and slapped him.

"Assault on an officer of the law," Rossiter said. "That won't sit well with a jury."

"Our lawyer will have us out of your jail in an hour," Liz said.

"Could be. That's something we'll have to find out." Rossiter pretended to see me for the first time. "Mr. Mallory, would you mind helping me with this arrest?"

"I'd be happy to," I said.

The next day it was time for me and Tess to leave. Sam was staying. He'd wired the Boss to let him know he was quitting the agency. I didn't know if he'd gotten a reply yet.

Tess wasn't sure she wanted to ride on the train with me.

"The last time I did that, you didn't take very good care of me," she said.

"I thought you could take care of yourself."

"I can. But you gave me a shanghai."

"I didn't give you a thing. You stole a drink from my flask. That was your mistake. Don't let it happen again."

I patted my coat pocket to make sure the flask was there. I didn't want to suffer a long train trip without some refreshment close at hand.

"What about that concussion?"

She was referring to the last time we'd worked together.

"That was your fault, too."

"I get the impression that you don't think much of my abilities, Dev."

"Well, you're wrong. I've seen you in action. Besides, you're the one who figured out that Harry was the one we were after."

"You're pretty slick, yourself. You conned those Hawes bitches twice."

"Such language."

"Do you think she's pretty? Liz Hawes?"

"She's beautiful. Why?"

She gave me a sideways look from beneath her eyelashes. "I was just wondering."

I felt awfully warm all of a sudden, and I was glad I had the flask along. I was going to need it. It looked to be a long trip back.